Copyright © 8/14/2020 Paris Cavanah

All rights reserved

The characters and events portrayed in this book are fictitious. Any similarity to real persons, living or dead, is coincidental and not intended by the author.

No part of this book may be reproduced, or stored in a retrieval system, or transmitted in any form or by any means, electronic, mechanical, photocopying, recording, or otherwise, without express written permission of the publisher.

ISBN: 9798576642823

Cover design by: Antonio Cesar
Editor: Terry Marshal
Library of Congress Control Number: 2018675309
Printed in the United States of America

To my husband, Bryce...for always loving me even when I'm acting crazy.

Thank you to my loving parents for teaching me from a young age that creativity is a precious gift.

Finally, thank you to all my readers and fans. Without you, my drive for perfection would not exist.

CONTENTS

Copyright
Dedication
Prologue — 3
A Very Strange Encounter — 6
Family Reunion — 27
Ron Shoves Me Into Space — 38
Another Alien Tries to Eat My Face — 59
I Find A Talking Bug — 74
A Dragon Karate Kicks My Face — 95
I Meet the New Chad Brunestick — 117
A Robot Beats Me Up In A Boxing Match — 140
I Join the Losers Club — 161
A Spider Shows Me I'm A Terrible Climber — 183
Corporal Vizen Sasses My Bullies — 198
My Flying Instructor Is A Chicken — 212
Ron And I Have A Death-Defying Space Race — 224

I Take A Road Trip to Creyenia	240
Gamirah Stands Up for Herself	262
We Get Our Butts Kicked By A Giant Tree	269
Girah Gets Some Free Remodeling	278
Turns Out, I'm a Crazy Person	290
Girit Gives Me a Solid Pep-Talk	299
This Isn't The End, Is It?!	303
Afterword	315
Books In This Series	317
Praise For Author	319
Acknowledgement	321

HYPERNOVA SERIES

A Trilogy About…

Love,

Family,

&

Discovering the Universe.

BY

PARIS CAVANAH

An Orphaned Bird Publication

PROLOGUE

When I was twelve years old, aliens abducted my brother Ron.

We snuck out of the house through the back-patio door on a dark, cold winter's night. I remember the yellow, overhanging streetlights illuminating the trees dusted with sprinkles of white powdered snow. Everything was silent, except for the soft sound of our boots crunching against the sidewalk. In the darkness, I held his hand tight as we crossed the road to the corner store a block away. For some reason, even back then, I knew everything would go wrong.

Ron made a type of Canadian tradition when we were kids. Go to the corner store, buy a Slurpee, then drink it in a minute. The two of us thought it was hilarious to watch the other get a brain freeze, both of our faces scrunched into tight balls of pain.

My brother always knew how to get us in trouble.

I always let him.

With our goodies in hand, we set out to walk home. The chilliness of the plastic cup frost-burned my bare palm. My eyes travelled down to the container, imagining how the flavours would taste. I picked lovely cherry, hypnotic blue crash, and Peps. For a second, time felt fluid as I stared down at the drink. Eventually, I looked back up at Ron's head as it bobbed happily back-and-forth.

That's when everything turned white ... zwipppp!

ZAP!

The cup slipped from my fingers into the snow, colouring the white surface red, pink, and blue. I tried to open my eyes but only got a glimpse before they slammed shut. The cold was unbearable; I called my brother's name until my throat was raw. A loud hummmmm made it impossible for him to hear. Ron's warm grip slipped from mine as the light began to diminish from beyond my sealed eyelids.

My eyes slowly opened. What I saw next haunted my dreams throughout my childhood.

A large silver saucer, hovering in the sky, shone a thick beam onto us. Ron, terrified and screaming, was rising up into the air towards the center of the ship.

I jumped. I tried to reach him. I tried to shout.

"Come back, Ron!! Come back!!"

But I was too small, too weak. Ron disappeared. So did the UFO, in a flash of brilliant rainbow lights.

I was left standing alone on the sidewalk, everything silent.

My memory gets hazy after that. I thought I heard somebody shouting my name.

"Ron? Where are you?" I screamed.

I was sure, at that moment, I would never see him again.

A VERY STRANGE ENCOUNTER

Alright, I'll admit it! Chad Brunestick is a jerk.

He wades in the pool with his two pals, staring with big, dumb grins. Chad's long blonde hair is flattened back tight, as though a bottle of cheap gel was poured onto it and his mother has slicked her fingers through the razor-sharp strands, attempting to feather down his unruly locks. Chad's brown eyes sparkle with energy; his stupid square chin is dotted with prickles of dark facial hair. He's always trying to show the girls his chin hairs as if to say, *'Look at me ladies, I'm a real man!'* I roll my eyes in disgust.

"Hey, Finn, what's the matter? Too chicken to swim?"

I stand at the side of the pool and cross my arms over my chest. My swim shorts are the same ones mom bought me when I was in grade seven. The bright blue tropical pattern is an eye-catching, yellowish-red spotted eyesore.

"Nobody asked for your opinion, Chad." I tell him

One of his flat-faced friends join in.

"Scared all the ladies are gonna see your skinny butt? Or smell your fish breath?"

Smirking, he nudges his friend on the shoulder.

"Ya! Who wants to date a dude with smelly breath?!"

They laugh like old women giggling over a romcom.

Idiots! I uncross my arms, as though my oversized white-t-shirt will act as armour against their sarcasm.

"Just go away. Don't you guys have anything better to do?"

Across the other side of the indoor swimming pool, Mr. Elk, the gym teacher, eyes up Chad's posse and begins walking to our side of the pool, mowing a path through kids who are unlucky enough to not get out of the way. I look down at my phone and plug in my earpieces, but Mr. Elk is a persistent man, built like the animal he is named after. He grabs the cord and, none too gently, pulls the earpieces out.

"Come on, Bates. Get in the pool. It's the last day before Christmas break. Show some effort."

Talk about not helping

I look back down at my bullies who have begun to swim away, kicking their feet up to send splashes of cold water in my direction. I close my eyes to shield them from the deluge.

Mr. Elk turns to them.

"Get out of here and back to the deep end!" he shouts, but the misfits are already several feet away.

Mr. Elk returns his gaze to me. I'm not sure what he sees, but I prepare for another order to *"Join in!"* Crap! It doesn't come, but his eyebrows scrunch and I can almost imagine steam rising from his ears. A couple of seconds pass and he just shrugs, and I watch him walk up to the rest of the class near the slide, barking out orders. Chad says something that makes the teacher laugh. I groan in genuine distaste.

Here's a million-dollar question. Why do people get bullied? What makes a bully? I can answer that question from first-hand experience. See, some individuals think it is a matter of bravery ...my father, for example. *'Finn, why don't you stand up for yourself? Son, if they land the first hit, you land one right back!'*

Not that easy! I stand up for myself all the time. For the last three years, in fact, but that makes you more of a target because bullying is a game for them.

Ok. So what makes a bully? Commonly, unfortunate living situations. They have it rough. They are the ones who are insecure, so they let their self-hatred and anger out on others.

I don't care. I hate them. As I said, Chad Brunestick is a jerk.

The school bell chimes fifteen minutes later. I rush into the boys' changing area before Chad and his pals have a chance to swim back and climb out of the pool to bother me. I grab my grey sweater, pulling up the hood while letting my black backpack slump over my shoulders.

My parents, despite my insistent arguments, forced me to go to school today. I have four more blocks to slog through after my encounter with Chad's boy band. I'm not in the mood for yet another day of mindless lecturing from my teachers. Besides, my parents also informed me I might not be going back to school after Christmas break. I have enough credits to graduate early. Jade Career College has accepted me into a twelve-week Astronomy course.

With this in mind, I run to my locker on the first floor.

The school is like a maze filled with scurrying rats. Before the next bell rings, I manage to clear my locker, shoving the contents into my bag. My notebooks, filled to the brim with scientific formulas and math equations, make up most of the bulk. Despite the weight, I manage to pull the straps neatly onto my back adjusting the pressure. I go to close my locker, but it magically swings shut with a bang!

Chad has his fist on the metal frame with a goofy smile stretching from ear to ear that he thinks is intimidating. I close my eyes, letting a wave of frustration pass.

"You know what's sad, Finn?"

I turn to look at him head-on.

"I don't care."

He continues anyway.

"This is the last day I get to hang out with you."

He punches my right arm. I flinch. He smirks, knowing that he must have left a little bruise.

"Don't touch me," I warn with a surprising amount of bravery.

This catches Chad off guard. He raises his brows.

"Tough guy now? Let me guess. You think going off to college will help you become cooler?"

Even an amateur can piece this mess together. *'Dumb tough guy is jealous of smart kid graduating early,'* Or maybe I'm giving myself to much credit. Either way, I turn around, walking towards the main entrance.

"You're so boring! Your brother would agree with me."

Chad's words roll over me like a warm wind across a valley. In my mind's eyes, I see Ron walking out of our bedroom, many years ago, his broad smile, glowing red cheeks, dark hair and chubby face send my heart into overdrive. I snap.

"Don't talk about my brother like that!"

My eyes burn, but no tears will come. I pivot, spittle flies free from my mouth with the vehemence of my retort.

"Have some decency!"

Chad goes chest to chest with me.

"Get over it, Finn. Ron disappeared five years ago." Chad chuckles. "Besides, I bet you get all the attention from your parents now that your big brother ain't coming back. Why the fuss dude?"

He shoves me square in the shoulders. I catch myself with my back heels, but the weight of my backpack betrays me, and I stumble onto the tiled floor.

Students around us begin to stare. Some pull out their phones snapping pictures and video. My face is burning, lips trembling, both hands clenched together, fisting. My bag slides from my back landing with a heavy thwack on the floor.

Chad has already begun his attack. He grabs me by the collar of my sweater, swinging me through the air. My laboured breath is knocked out of my lungs as I make contact with the solid metal of my locker.

"What's the matter?! Can't fight back, four eyes?"

Adrenaline is coursing through my veins, heavy and thick, lubricating my joints, powering my leg muscles. I kick the inside of Chad's knee, hard. He stumbles back, giving me room for leverage. I propel myself off the lockers; he hits the floor on his back with me on top—*payback time.*

Raising my fist, the image of landing a hit right between Chad's eyes makes my arm shake. My nails dig into the palm of my hand as I clench my fist angling my shot.

My hesitation costs me. Bam! Chad's fist impacts the curve of my chin. I stand up, shocked. He starts to follow, but a female teacher, Miss Scarlet, makes her way towards us. Her eyes narrow and she approaches us with short, powerful strides, forced by her pencil dress.

"What is going on?!" she demands.

So, I do what I always do. Grab my backpack, turn tail and run.

Miss Scarlett yells my name as I barrel out the front doors towards the bus loop that serves the city center.

"Finn Bates! You get back here right now!" she shouts but her voice is receding as I hurtle onwards.

I don't look back. Right now, all I'm thinking about is the night I lost my brother. *Why does Chad have to be so fat-headed? Making me feel like this...*

With four blocks between myself and Bayside Senior High, my legs are tiring, and I need a pause. My bag drops from my shoulders into a heap on the sidewalk. A little dot of red draws my gaze to my hand. Gingerly I examine it. The wounds from my nails digging in are minor at best.

No way I'm going home now...Mom and Dad will kill me. The thought depresses me. *Not like they won't anyway...* Recognizing the inevitable confrontation facing me, I hoist up my bag and start walking home once again.

The morning cold still lies thick in the air. I readjust my baggy hood, putting in my earpieces and opting to listen to some old-time blues to calm my nerves. *Look on the bright side! At least this is your last day of High School.* While I walk, reality battles against my optimism.

Sure...but now you're going to have a bunch of college kids hating you because you're some young prodigal genius. Shut up brain. Just focus on the music; let the artist's deep raspy voice accompanied by a string guitar distract me from my anxieties. *Home is not where I want to be right now. Maybe Lolly lake would be a better place to spend the afternoon.* I head into the city center, which is the fastest way to get to the eastern road that leads to the outskirts of town.

My town, Bayside Heights, is well-populated, yet still considered country living. We have a dense core filled with large malls and shops, while picket-fenced neighbourhoods, surrounded by acres of land, are scattered atop the rolling hills. Home is on one of these hills, where I live with my mother and father, who, amongst other things, are absent in my day-to-day life.

That's what happens when aliens abduct their eldest son! I come to a halt at a red pedestrian light until the familiar walk signal beckons me. *How many times do I need to tell myself this? Aliens didn't abduct Ron...it was just how the car's headlights shone in the night.*

Yet, in my memory, I can see the whitish-blue

beam, clear as day. It shone down from the clouds like an unearthly beacon, lifting my fifteen-year-old brother in the air. It left me crying and alone on that cold winter's night.

Ya ya, poor kid! That's so sad. Moving on.

Last month, I turned seventeen, so I still hold many of my 'baby face' features from when I was younger. My short, curly black hair weaves curlicues around my ears with thicker strands on my forehead. Behind my wide-rimmed glasses, perched delicately on my nose, are two dark green eyes. Not a face to excite the opposite sex, which is why Chad's taunt still stings.

Reaching the Jade Forest perimeter, I look around. Behind me, at the bottom of the hill, the cars and people create hypnotic lines, blurring the road like worker ants. The distance from my problems comforts me, settling me back into a calm state of mind.

My eyes wander up into the vast canopy to soak up the atmosphere. I get off the main road onto a dirt path, stomped flat by the feet of many hikers. Slowly, I remove my earpieces. Birds chirp a simple chorus. A white butterfly brushes past the tip of my nose, probably on a late migration. The tree branches reach out to hug me, brushing against my arms and feet. A bug, on a nearby branch, flashes across my vision. I let my eyes wander into a bush that it jumped to.

A pair of large white eyes stare at me from between the branches. Goosebumps race up both arms. Those eyes are animalistic. I blink several times. When my vision clears, the mysterious creature is gone.

My heart trips in my chest, playing a drumbeat in my ears. The pounding makes it hard to hear. I strain to catch any possible sound...yet there is nothing. The shock slowly wears off. I straighten my back, still tense. I have to wonder, *did I really see anything?*

Is my mind playing tricks on me? Maybe I'm insane, or Chad is still getting to me. Dismissing myself as mildly delusional takes the edge off.

Reaching Lolly Lake, I smile down at the small ripples of clear blue water oozing up through the dark grey sand. To my left, the main beach stretches out, abandoned during the cold months. The landscape reminds me of an oil painting. Thick leaves intermix with pine needles, blending in shadows of green, brown, and yellowish-orange earthy tones. Forest smells tickle my nose along with the refreshing breath of the lake. Beyond the beach, a mountain tries to hide behind the clouds. The range pierces the sky as the sun sends rays of warmth towards me.

Living on the West Coast, we don't get snow during winter. Perhaps on rare occasions, a storm will hit, but it is nothing that won't be cleared in a day or two. Instead, we get rain; lots and lots of rain.

Gazing at the lake, I see a clear reflection of my face and Chad's comments return to haunt me. I stare in disdain at the sight of the flushed pale skin of my cheeks. But at that very moment, the clouds part and it begins to rain. In the lake water, the droplets ripple as they race across the surface, skewing my reflection and washing it away.

I take shelter under the canopy of a large cedar, settling down on the sand, staring up at the sky, and letting my mind clear...

Shuffle... Blinking twice while adjusting my glasses, I stand up and nervously scan the forest. The foliage no longer feels safe. With the rain coming down harder, the shadows dance, deepening to hide who-knows-what.

"Grrrrr..."

Ok, so I'm not crazy. There is something in the woods. The ground bruises my knee as I drop to rip open my backpack. The bear spray I want will have ended up under all my books...

Finally! It's in my hand and my arm comes free...

"Grrrr!"

The noise is coming from behind me. A shiver runs through me. *It can't be more than a few feet away?*

I peek over my shoulder, my heart jams in my throat.

A large canine head pushes through the low branches and undergrowth. It is three times the size of any wolf I have ever seen. The upper branches crack, the leaves brush off its fur coat. *My god, it's the size of a car!* For all of its size, the monster's paws make no sound as it steps onto the beach. Razor-sharp teeth gleam from its maw. Two white holes stare at me where its eyes would be, spiralling up to the top of its flat head, turning into points next to tiny ears. From its furry haunches, two thin tails split apart, rotating clockwise while it continues to eye me up as a meal.

What the heck is this monster!?

It dawns on me quickly. *Right! I have no flippin' clue.*

I cautiously get up, holding the bear mace in my trembling hand. The raindrops sink into its short fur as if it is an absorbent sponge. Meanwhile, I need a set of windshield wipers for my glasses. I attempt to rub away the water with the back of my hand. Those white eyes follow my movement. The giant beast takes a step towards me, growling as it comes.

With my finger trembling on the trigger of the mace, every part of me shakes uncontrollably. My heart right now would outpace a jackhammer and I know I'm pale as a ghost. Its power shifts to its hind legs, and it leaps.

"No!!" My heart beats so hard it might explode and, instinctively, I duck!

"BANG!!"

△△△

The monster sails over my crouched body. Smoke mixed with burnt fur, fouling the air. The beast lands poorly, air rushing from its lungs while kicking sand back into my face. I spit out the grit, staring at the beast's wounds.

Is that a...a burn? On its hind leg? The size of a football!

"Well, ugly? You want another piece of me?!" a low voice says from the woods.

A tall, rangy figure, emerges from the forest. Medium wavy black hair is slicked behind his ears. A grin plays on his square face. On the left side of his chin, travelling down the base of his neck, are faded burns that mar and twist his clear skin. His brown eyes glimmer. In his hands is some sort of gun. The tip of his weapon fizzles, crackling with electricity. It looks like a blaster from some kind of sci-fi movie.

The monster growls again, rising to its paws. Its twin tails whip-snap, lighting fast as it leaps towards the stranger. He steps onto the beach, salsa dancing around the creature. The monster's head slams into a tree. The stranger fires again. A sickening burning smell of singed fur and seared flesh waft over us from the monster's hide. It is the finishing blow. The creature howls, falling over, bursting into a cloud of gray-ash that is quickly washed away by the heavy rainfall.

I stand, staring at the stranger. My eyes have to be as wide as saucers. I raise the bear mace towards him.

"Wh- who are you!?" I hiss.

His eyebrows furrow, lips clamping together. He's wearing a long-sleeved wool sweater that's tight against his strong arms, and a dark green down-vest that falls past his hips, partially hiding a black leather belt. His blue jeans are tucked into a pair of boots.

"Just calm down."

His voice is deep and has a calming tone. He presses a button on the hilt of his gun, the snap-crackle of electricity winks out as the muzzle folds towards the trigger, creating a compact silver square which he shoves into his back pocket.

"I'll be honest; I wasn't expecting to have this conversation here."

He takes a step. My stomach churns. *What can he want with me?* I step back until the heel of my left foot digs into the mud at the lake's edge.

My mind is reeling.

"What was that monster!?" I shout.

"It was a Spawn-"

He looks at the bear mace still in my hands.

"L-let's just put down the bear mace, ok?"

I shake my head.

"What's a Spawn?"

He takes another step, then stops.

"Listen, Finn; we should talk about this over a cup of coffee."

He gives a small smile, moving within three feet of me. *Well, I was thinking of trusting you until you said my name.*

"How do you know who I am? Are you stalking me?"

He tries to reach for my bear mace.

Bad move weirdo!

I aim below his chest, squeezing the trigger. He yelps, jumping away from me. Despite my fear induced panic, I avoid nailing him in the face. I scoop my bag out of the sand, running into the forest, wanting nothing more than to go home, forgetting any of this happened.

That monster was probably just in my imagination...yes, a nightmare!

When my feet hit the road, I turn left. Parked several feet away, is an old Honda Civic.

As I am about to run past it, an irresistible feeling of curiosity overcomes me. I peek through the dirty windows. Empty pizza boxes and fast-food bags litter the passenger's seat floorboards. A sanitized smell mixed with a scent that reminds me of moms cleaning polish intermixes with the trash. Glowing shiny metal balls, the size of my fist lay partially covered by a pizza box and a fast-food wrapper. What appear to be brass knuckles with short, curved blades extended from each end lie in view beside it.

All sorts of spy thriller plots race through my mind. *Maybe, he works for the Canadian intelligence services. What about the American's? Could he be FBI, CIA?* As crazy as it sounds, the glowing metal balls remind me of something I saw in "Men In Black". *I must be going crazy.*

No time to think, I need to get to the police and make

a statement in case there are any more creatures around.

Charging down the hill, I make a beeline into town. My hood flaps like a flag in a windstorm. The breeze pushes mounting sweat from my forehead.

The police station's red roof and brown trim comes into view. I race up the front steps, whipping the door open. The sound of them slamming against the wall echoes in counterpoint to my panting in the previously quiet room.

A friend of my father, Officer Charles, is sitting at the entry desk with a coffee cup. The disgruntled frown on his face makes the fat around his chin sag.

"Finn Bates? What's the matter, kid?" he mumbles while swallowing his last gulp.

I run to the desk, catching my breath.

"In-" I huff and puff "-the woods!"

"You see a bear?"

He raises his voice, putting down his empty paper cup; the bottom leaves an instant circular stain on his notes and papers.

"Finn, I can't count how many times I've told ya. Stay out a' the forest this time of year."

Shaking my head, I'm finally able to catch my breath.

"No! A real monster! It looked like a wolf, with two tails, huge eyes and sharp teeth!"

I spread my arms as wide as they will go.

"Only bigger," I gasp

Charles's eyebrows raise. His skeptical look heats my blood. *It's the same look dad, and mom gave me when Ron disappeared.*

"Finn, there are no such things as monsters."

My adrenaline is still running high and I prattle on, hoping he will understand.

"I was attacked, then this man showed up with a gun!"

Charles frowns as he grabs a piece of paper; I realize...

He doesn't believe me. I slump against the counter. *Why would he? I must sound like a maniac.* I pinch the bridge of my nose then step away from the desk.

At six feet, Charles towers over me. His lips are set in a straight line.

"I heard you got in a fight today Finn; maybe you're just having an episode."

I glare up at him as he continues.

"Why don't you…"

"No…"

I try to summon up the last of my patience. *If he doesn't believe me, maybe my parents will.* It's a slim chance, but it's what I have to work with.

"I'm feeling better now."

In my haste, I stumble into the door. Charles offers to give me a ride home.

"You don't look fit to be walking around Finn."

My falling against the door pushes the handle. There is a satisfying click, the door opens, and a cold breeze draws me onto the rainy sidewalk.

"Sorry for bothering you--"

I twist, scurrying to the nearest crosswalk, still in panic mode. The rain soaks my hair and face.

Before I get very far, someone shouts from behind me.

"Finn! Please stop-"

That wasn't Office Charles.

I peek over my shoulder.

"No.."

There in the street is the stranger. He must have driven up when I left the police station. His window is down. He pulls up into the nearest parking spot and leans out the window. Before I can say anything, he shouts.

"Please!"

His hand grips the top of the door. It's trembling.

The desperation in his voice freezes me. That shout, it's familiar. My heart gets yanked by an invisible string. This time, I don't run. Slowly, I walk towards his car.

Bystanders stare at us from across the street. The man hanging from the car window catches sight of the gawkers.

"I'm supposed to be under cover" he says.

He closes his eyes, running his free hand through his hair as though combing the frustration out. When he opens his eyes again, that broad smile, calm demeanor and childish stare are now five years older than I remember, but I know this man.

"Ron?"

FAMILY REUNION

"As I said," he whispers. "I didn't want this meeting to be so abrupt."

I don't know what to say. My stomach is still in knots. I take another step away from him. Ron takes a deep breath, opening the car door and closing it behind him. He follows as I hesitantly back-pedal onto the sidewalk.

My tongue finally unravels from the disbelief of this strange revelation.

"My brother disappeared years ago; you can't be him."

"I am." he declares. "Just, please don't spray me with mace again, ok?"

I ignore his plea.

"Really? Prove you're my brother."

"I will, but over a cup of Joe. It's freezing out here."

In silence we walk half a block to the "Java Coffee Bar", one of the better places in town. It's virtually deserted at this time of day. Heidi, the cute little waitress, comes over and I see Ron eyeing her appreciatively.

"What can I get you guys?" she asks.

"Just two large coffees and lots of sugar" Ron says

"I'll be right back," she says and heads back to the counter with Ron's eyes following her all the way.

I hear the hiss of the coffee dispenser and, in moment she returns with two
steaming mugs and a pile of sugar sachets. When she has gone (and because I'm now convinced that it is him) I leave Ron time to sugar and stir his coffee before I rest my arms on the table.

Leaning in, my jaw tightens. I can see my reflection in Ron's eyes. I can't tell what he's thinking, but I assume he's surprised at my measured tones. But he's still Ron, and I know he cares.

"Tell me what happened, now that I know that you're Ron without a doubt."

"Without a doubt, huh?"

His shoulders relax, eyes close.

"That night...a group of Raiders captured me.

They go by many names. You can refer to them as space pirates if you want."

I want to ask why they took him and not me, but I am sure that all of my questions will be answered if I'm patient.

"These Raiders travel across the galaxies, committing illegal acts for the highest bidders. The ship that abducted me was travelling to Disclosed Planets and capturing their native species."

I am struck by the sadness in his eyes. This memory clearly pains him.

"A Disclosed Planet is like Earth. It's a place that hasn't been deemed worthy to join in on the rest of the expanding universe."

"The rest..of the universe?" I repeat in awe.

He gazes back outside, but not at the sky or the roads. Beyond that, towards the stars.

"Earth is still considered an infant planet, not technologically advanced enough to comprehend the wonders that are up in space, Finn. Thousands of light-years away are millions of planets occupied by species of life incredibly diverse, yet beautifully unique."

Ron's eyes are alight with wonder. When he turns back, it infects me. I can vividly imagine what he must see; millions of planets dancing across the infinite expanse of space.

I want to tell him how I feel, but he continues.

"When they stole me away, I was locked up in a cold cell on a foreign ship, alongside scary alien lifeforms, but I noticed right away that they were as intelligent as you or I. Even more so in many cases, but we were all united by one thing. We wanted to escape and we planned hard to do so."

He raises his right hand, giving a sad smile as his finger traces the burn marks along his face.

"Let's just say our plan backfired...no pun intended."

He tries to make light of what emotionally scars him.

"Nobody else made it out but me, because I was saved."

"Saved, by who?"

"The Citadel."

"Who are they?" I ask.

"The Citadel is a confederation of sentient creatures that are the groundwork of law and order in all of the Known Galaxies. They recruit only the strongest, bravest and most loyal species from accepted planets to train at one of their five

Outposts. Citadel members are real heroes. They train hard from a young age to learn how to fight, to protect against Raiders, scavengers, and thieves. They also try to raise Disclosed Planets, like Earth, towards their level of understanding. They can only do that by entrusting members of the resident species to work for them...in secret, to prove that planet's worth."

Work. In secret? I think I'm starting to piece this together.

"What did they do after they saved you?"

Ron's chin lifts, a quirky smile on the corner of his mouth.

"Well, Citadel rules state that if an individual from a Disclosed Planet encounters any alien life form, they can never go home."

I gasp, shaking my head. Ron tries to hold his smile, but it's fading once more.

"So just because you got swept up in the mess of those Raiders, you couldn't come home?"

Ron tries to explain himself.

"You can't blame the Citadel, Finn. You don't understand. The fabric of the universe balances on the tip of a pin."

He gestures to the sky.

"If our planet discovered the truth of what lies beyond, what do you think we would do?"

I instantly think about people like Chad Brunestick, I mumble.

"I...dont know."

"Exactly! After what I saw up there, could you blame me?"

"Blame you for what?" I whisper.

Ron bites his lower lip.

"They made me a deal that if I work for them long enough; if I can prove that humans are capable of working with The Citadel, that's when they'll agree to make the earth a Known Planet, and boom!-", he claps his hands together, "I'll finally come home..."

The information Ron has given me is a lot to digest. I put my elbows on the table, setting my chin on the base of my palms, and turn towards the window. Rain still falls, creating puddles in the parking lot. The gentle splashes help me relax, sorting through these new facts.

"So, the universe is filled with aliens, and you joined the space police?" I say matter-of-factly.

My eyes trail over to his burns, which appear darker under the hanging lights.

"They won't let you go home until you prove Earth is good enough to join their ranks?"

Ron's gaze grows stern, his mouth a straight line, jaw tight.

"I wanted to call, maybe send a message but I couldn't." he says despondently. "I'm so sorry."

My heart aches.

"It's ok, Ron."

For the first time, I genuinely smile at him.

"What do you need me to do?"

He can't believe what he's hearing.

"R-really?"

I nod.

"Mom and Dad, they haven't been the same without you. If I can bring you home...maybe, things will be like they used to be?"

"What do you mean by, 'how they used to be'?"

I try to read the expression on his face. He looks curious, but a looming sense of sadness lingers around that dejected frown.

I know the truth.

I won't tell him Mom and Dad don't talk to me anymore. Mom quit her job as a waitress a few months ago; now, she stays at home, puttering over everyday chores, then locking herself in her bedroom. Dad is always travelling abroad, never bothering to say 'hello' or 'goodbye.' We all feel completely disassociated from one another, locked up in our problems in this big evil world.

I imagine what it is going to be like for Ron to hear all of this, to know that his family is falling apart because of his disappearance.

I can't tell Ron we've become a damaged home. It'll break his heart.

Instead, I spin the facts into a true-ish statement.

"Mom works at home now, Dad makes lots of money travelling abroad, so we're kind of spoiled. I'm wrapped up in my studies, so we don't hang out as much as we used to when you and I were kids, but that's just what happens when you grow up."

I shrug, like it's no big deal, then smile.

"We still care about each other, though. It's just a little different."

Ron's eyes settle. He leans back in his chair, a playful grin on his face as he lets out a heartfelt sigh.

"I'm so glad to hear that. I would hate it if they were upset and couldn't move on."

"Go on then." I give an eager push. "Tell me the rest."

That's when Heidi returns with the coffee pot and gives us refills.

"Anything else I can get you?" She asks.

"How about some fries to share?" I suggest.

She puts the notepad into her apron, looking at Ron curiously before glancing over at me.

She nods and heads back to the counter.

I turn to Ron, hoping he will finish his narrative.

"Lately, the Citadel has been landed with a problem. New Scavengers and Raiders have been appearing all over the galaxy, stealing and attacking Known planets, along with Disclosed planets. Currently, our available fleets are outnumbered. We need recruits. Worst of all, we've heard rumors of a new mysterious enemy cloaked in darkness. Stories call him or her, Odium"

My logical brain begins searching for a meaning behind the name. *Doesn't Odium mean hate?*

"The Citadel believes that this dark-figure has something to do with the attacks."

I sip the hot coffee without sugar or cream. Ron raises an eyebrow.

"Aren't you a little young for coffee?"

I smile. "I'm seventeen, dude."

He gives a knowing nod.

"On top of all that grief, Raiders and villains alike are taking keen interest in planets like Earth. More Spawn seem to be circulating, sneaking onto planets that haven't been approved by the Citadel."

"What on earth is a Spawn?" I ask.

"Oh, right! Imagine it's like a 'space mosquito' They come from a minor galaxy in the far reaches of space. We suspect that they have become allied somehow with Odium who has encouraged them to blindly attack any life forms they can get their paws on. It was thought that they acted purely instinctively, but we are seriously concerned now that they've started showing strategic planning...calculated attacks... more proof, perhaps, that they have come under Odium's influence."

"Wow. So, you guys have your hands full huh?"

One more sip of my coffee. He stares at me with a soft grin.

"I wish I could help." I mutter. His grin explodes.

"That's why I'm here. Finn. Do you want to join

The Citadel?"

RON SHOVES ME INTO SPACE

"What about Mom and Dad, when they realise that their other son is gone?"

My voice fills with concern.

"Ron, I want to help, but disappearing from my life here completely?"

Ron shakes his head.

"No, Finn, you'll be a special case, the only one of your kind."

I can't keep the doubt out of my voice.

"How am I going to be unique? Aren't you a human too?"

His voice drops to a whisper.

"I am, but I've been told that I need assistance in

making Earth a Known Planet. You'll work but study around a personal schedule. The Citadel already knows you graduated early; you'll have plenty of free time."

He's talking a mile a minute. I'm surprised he has a second to catch his breath.

"We need to recruit somebody new, a human that is smart, caring, and up to such a momentous task. I told my higher-ups that person was you."

Self-doubt courses through me. *I wouldn't call myself any of those things. I don't care about Chad; I don't have any friends. I'm smart, but not the most intelligent on the planet. I can't write an essay to save my life. My English teacher Mrs. Pratt will vouch for that!*

"Ron, that's high praise n' all but..."

The hope in his eyes lingers.

"I'm not a hero. Honestly, the idea of fighting another Spawn scares me."

"You can train Finn; you won't be alone. You will be guided, taught to be an amazing "Fledgil", which is what they call new recruits."

His voice is serious again.

"Besides, I remember you as the kid on the block who was always willing to help others. What about that kid who broke his leg at the Big Red

Slide park? What was his name? You remember. You carried him to his house despite-the-fact he weighed twice as much as you." He snaps his fingers a few times. "Simon! That was it."

I grasp my hot cup, letting the warmth soothe me.

"I know. It's just ...sometimes, I don't feel like the same kid I used to be."

Everything in my childhood is painted with such brilliance and warmth, but when our parents started to close themselves off, so did I. Everything turned blue and grey. Memories filled with paperwork, along with late nights staring at my ceiling, wondering if I could be happy again.

Ron's is so enthusiastic that I start to think that maybe the colour can return to my life. *Do I have it in me to change the world? Five years ago I would have said yes!*

Ron waits, his face, nervous and tight. One of his feet taps against the floor while his hands knit together in anticipation.

"I'll do it."

Whether this works out or not, I need to change something in my life! I won't pass up this opportunity. One day, I'll make Mom smile like she used to, and Dad will finally want to come home!

"Really!? You mean it?"

I am surprised to find myself nodding. Ron's grin splits his face.

"I- I mean, heck ya. Finn, that's amazing!"

I, too, am grinning from ear to ear.

"Just tell me where to start."

△△△

The young waitress returns to place a large plate of fries on the table between us. Ron eats ninety percent of them. I don't bother interrupting his feast.

"I haven't had Earth food for so long! It's so good."

"Why not order something else?"

He shakes his head.

"I have so much to show you before today ends; no time for food!"

He shovels the fries into his mouth while I fill him in about my studies, and the University I would have been attending.

"You won't lose out, I promise. You'll get to learn what an adventurous life is truly like."

Our waitress arrives with the bill and a debit machine. Ron smiles.

"I'll pay"

He pulls out a watch with silver trim. A black squid (or maybe it's an octopus?) is etched on the face below a row of alien inscriptions.

The waitress looks puzzled.

"This machine has tap, but I don't think we accept that kind of payment?"

Ron taps the debit machine with the watch and it pings "Approved".

"Oh!" she gasps.

Her eyes light up. Ron must have given her a large tip.

Leaving the diner, we make our way back to his beat-up car. The rain is still pouring down. The water and mud on the bottom of my shoes begin to freeze my toes. When we reach Ron's car, I get in the passenger's seat.

Ron notices how soaked I am.

"I got some fresh socks n' a sweater back on my ship."

"You have a ship? Like, a spaceship?" I gasp.

"Ya, man."

He rolls up his sweater sleeve, revealing once

again his extraordinary silver watch.

"Is that a fit-bit?"

Ron laughs, shaking his head.

"It's a Jericho Watch."

He raises the face to the front of the steering wheel and the car's motor springs to life.

"This car was made at Citadel H.Q., especially for this undercover job," he explains while pulling out of the parking lot. "I needed to fit in, unobtrusively, and this seemingly old junker doesn't attract attention but it has a few hidden tricks up its sleeve!"

Immediately, I piece-together how Ron managed to catch up to me after our encounter in the forest. My brother drives like a maniac, not using his indicator, speeding through yellow lights. My sweaty palms grip the dashboard for dear life.

Speeding through the downtown core, we leave the outskirts, ending up on the other side of the city. Humble homes and apartments decorated with flowers zoom past. Ron taps the face of his Jericho Watch.

Skkkkirrrrtttt!

The car comes to an abrupt halt on the side of the road, outside the Big Red Slide Park, aptly named for its large slide that cascades down a steep hill, opening up at a playground next to a large field.

In the sudden silence, I hear the steady plunk--plunk--plunks– of rain on the steel roof of the car.

"My ship is in that field."

He points down the hill. I survey the empty surroundings but can see nothing.

"Must be a tiny ship!

He laughs at that, opening his door. I follow while he responds.

"Gotta get with the program Finn. It's cloaked."

I stare at him in disbelief as we stand atop the hill. My mind floods with fond memories of playing hide-seek, grounders, and red rover with Ron and the other neighbourhood kids in this park. Now, the place is abandoned, the Elementary School torn down and the once thriving neighbourhood left vacant for low-income residents.

"Careful" Ron warns. "The hill is slippery."

We start our descent.

"How long have you been on Earth?" I ask him

"Just got here last night. Slept in my ship n' tracked you down this morning."

The storm is getting worse. My cheap backpack is

leaking out from the bottom, soaking my jeans.

Good thing I won't be needing that homework...

Once on flat land, I follow Ron's muddy tracks to the edge of the field. He stops suddenly and I almost skid into his backside. He pulls out his watch, tapping the screen. A holographic interface expands from his wrist. Several folder emojis appear and he swipes through them with his finger, reaching a symbol that looks like a spaceship. He taps it, the Jericho Watch emits a blip!

Several feet in front of us, a wave of energy pulses, seemingly from nowhere. The pulses intensify and I find myself staring at the huge shape of Ron's ship.

"This is an older E-O-N ship model crafted by Citadel students themselves and equipped especially for this trip. I call her Eunoia."

Eunoia is around a hundred feet wide and as tall as a three-story building. It is oval-shaped, tapering at the front end to where what looks like a conventional windshield is inset. It is matte-black.

Ron sees my astonishment.

"The coating is a highly advanced form of the non-reflective finish Earth developed for its Stealth aircraft. It is vital that my trip here isn't detected."

"But if the ship is cloaked, it's invisible, right?"

Then a thought comes to me.

"Wait a minute! You are cloaked, as in...invisible, but you still have mass that could possibly be detected by radar, hence the reflective coating. Man, that's so cool."

"See! I always knew you were the brightest kid on the block," Ron grins.

I spot a wing folded against Eunoia's side and imaging that there is one on the other side also. Projecting beyond the rear of the ship are twin engines. They are fat and bulky, unlike any that I have ever seen before. There is also a sharp tailplane that looks like a fashion accessory rather than a functioning piece of mechanical equipment. The ship is so enormous that I can't see any of its top features from here.

Squinting, I continue to survey for a way in. *Is this hunk of junk gonna fly?*

The ship ripples.

"Step back a bit bro'"

I do as Ron says. He taps his watch, and a door on the right-hand side of the right-wing glides aside, allowing a gentle white glow from inside to illuminate the rain like glitter. A silver ramp, straight out of the UFO textbook, emerges from the base of the door, coasting down to level with the grass.

"Follow me," Ron calls.

My stomach clenches and I gulp air before stepping onto the ramp. My brother walks casually into the ship, but this is all new to me, so I move much more cautiously. I find myself in a windowless space about the size of a small boxroom, with a door in the opposite wall.

"This is an airlock under normal circumstances," Ron tells me, "but as we are at 'earth normal', we don't need to worry."

He taps his watch. The ramp slides up into its storage area and the exterior door slides closed. There is a slight hiss as it seals.

He leads me through the portal on the other side of the airlock into a large metal-lined room. Tubes run along the back wall. Beneath them are a series of metal boxes filled with mechanical equipment, some recognizable but much of it completely alien.

Ron crosses to a door set with an oval-shaped window.

"Check this out, Finn" he says.

I join him and gaze through the window. All I see is a huge empty space.

"So, what am I looking at?" I ask him.

"Past this door is an airlock leading to the docking bay" he tells me. "Eunoia can carry two fighter craft at a time. She's a model built mainly for transportation and delivery missions, but she can defend herself as well, if need be."

He presses a point on his Jericho Watch, which lights up. He looks down at it as if checking the time.

"Come on," he waves. "The fun stuff is upstairs on the main deck"

He turns towards a metal ladder that climbs several feet up the end wall. Air hisses around me, causing the hairs on my arms to stand on end.

"It's just Eunoia's AI re-calibrating the pressure." he grins.

I grab onto the ladder and start to climb. Above me, he cracks open a hatch into another room. He steps up into it, turns and reaches out his hand. I take it, and he pulls me up.

This space is phenomenal! The vast area is packed with more mechanical equipment emitting strange sounds. Tubes and wires are clamped against the walls, coming together at the entrance to a large conduit at ceiling level into which they all disappear. On the northern and southern walls are long blue sofas. The closest has a mess of pillows and blankets heaped on it. In the middle of the room, a table with a holographic top that shines a brilliant light, projecting a strange-looking creature over the table.

"What is that?" I ask. "An alien?"

"Close.", Ron says. "It is a Kraken and it identifies our craft. You could say it's our logo."

Even as I watch, the holographic image morphs into an attractive female who announces:

"Systems check complete. All ship functions are go."

Staring with amazement, I approach the table, swiping my hand through the air, harmlessly passing through the image.

"As I said earlier, Eunoia is equipped with an A.I system. I got to create her image and I named her EON." Ron proudly declares. "I wanted you to meet her. Mostly, though, you'll just hear her.

"You created her?" I gasp.

"Well, yes. She may be just a hologram, but she is often the only company I have on a long mission, so she might as well be attractive. Mind you, being an AI, she thrashes me at chess any time we play."

I'm at a loss for words so I look around and notice an in-wall mini-fridge covered with stickers and photos. Making my way towards them, I stare. *Is that a huge dragon-like alien standing next to Ron? And that looks like a thank you note, written in crayon?* "Dear Ron, thank you for delivering my package on such short notice. I'm sure my fifty children will love their new speidels and crammels!"

All I can do is boggle at the idea of any creature fathering fifty children.

"Hey, Finn, over here!"

Like a ringmaster, he gestures towards his next act.

"These are our storage chests."

There are a number of in-wall dark-grey cabinets, each with a large blue button on the front. At a touch, they glide open. Ron opens the first one to reveal four drawers. The top one is filled with files and textbooks written in an alien language. The next has shirts, pants, and socks. The third and fourth are empty.

"The other lockers are empty too. I like to keep most of my personal belongings on Altair."

He digs into the drawer, pulling out a fresh pair of white socks. He throws them at me.

"I didn't bring my sneakers. Sorry. Besides, I'm sure we ain't the same shoe size."

I look down at my tiny feet, wiggling my toes.

He grabs a large white t-shirt throwing it over to me. The shirt lands awkwardly in the crook of my arms. I unfold it and gulp. A little green alien holding a purple drink is smiling at me with his thumb up, some sort of catch-phrase is written in yellow.

"What the..."

"What?"

"N...Nothing! Looks great."

Look on the bright side; at least it's clean. Ron moves along, oblivious to my hesitation, gesturing at a large blue and white locker the size of our kitchen on the back wall.

"This is the big finale."

Ron places his eye on the retinal scanner. A blue light glimmers while EON chimes:

"Recognition complete! Weapons locker access confirmed."

The barrier slides left, clicking into place. I stare at the mass of equipment hanging from the hooked shelves. Blue bombs like those in his Honda are packaged in a case at the bottom of the locker, while two guns, different from the one he was carrying earlier, rest above. They look similar, like handguns, with round plated barrels connected to a trio of wires running to the grip and trigger.

"That's a Photon Blaster and," he says, pointing, "those are Argon Bombs!"

It sounds like a bunch of gibberish to me. I stand beside Ron, and reach out to pick up a weapon and get the feel of it. Before I barely make a move, the weapons locker snaps closed, almost chopping off my fingers.

Ron grins.

"You are not authorized to have access yet. That will come later."

A strange smell catches my attention causing my nostrils to flare, *Pepperoni? Cheese?* On the table, I spot a square box containing a single slice of green pizza.

"Is that pizza?"

Ron's dirty napkins lie next to it, soaked in grease. I have to fight the urge, to find a trash bin and start cleaning. Ron looks over and grins.

"Nah- it's an individual Grok meat meal from a few galaxies over, so ya, it's pizza."

Walking over to one of the lockers, I place my ruined bag down. I hear Ron play with the control panel as I switch out my socks, replacing my wet sweater and undershirt with the new ones he gave me.

"Time for us to head for the flight deck. Come on." Ron says.

He walks back towards the ladder and I realize that it continues upwards. He goes ahead and I follow him into a much smaller area that houses two seats that look like those you might find on the flight deck of any modern passenger jet. He takes the left hand one and motions for me to occupy the other one. But that is where the likeness ends. The blanked-out windshield is in front of us but below that is a simple panel that houses several banks of switches and what appears to be a radar screen but is infinitely more complex. Beside it is a system information screen.

He flips a switch, and the systems screen indicates that the ship's AI is active.

""EON, let's take this nice n' easy. Park us outside of earth's thermosphere!" Ron orders.

"Affirmative. Coordinates set." comes EON's soft female voice.

"Wait, hold up! We're leaving now? But I didn't pack!" I protest.

"Don't panic; it's just a test drive!"

He flips a switch and the windshield turns clear. The park rests peacefully thirty feet below.

We begin to rise. There is no sound and I

wouldn't have known it but
my chair shakes gently and I see the ground beginning to recede.

"How on earth?..." I gasp.

"Anti-gravitics." Ron says. "Many alien systems have had it for centuries. It provides a controllable means of converting gravitational attraction into repulsion. It is fitted mainly to Citadel freighters that need to land on other planets. Fighters don't need them since they operate in space."

We accelerate and The Big Red Slide Park turns into a speck in my vision, then disappears completely. *I think I'm going to be sick!*

My fingers squeeze so tight, the knuckles pop as I suck in a deep breath. The ship pivots, and my view of the ground is obliterated by rain splattering against the windshield. Dark clouds race towards us. We hit a wall of turbulence within the storm; a giggle escapes my lips just before we punch through the grey rain into a dark eclipse above the Earth's stratosphere. I am aware that space-sickness is a common phenomenon but I never expected to feel it myself. I squeeze my eyes shut and manage to hold in my stomach contents as the ship hums to a standstill.

"It's ok, Finn. You can open your eyes now."

I do as he says.

We shifted while my eyes were closed. Eunoia is now facing the Earth and the view is almost impossible to put it into words. The rays from the sun hit earth directly. I see millions of dazzling lights, every colour imaginable. Rose-coloured dots speckle the horizon. Iridescent clumps of forest intertwine across the peaks of mountain formations. Beyond that, I see mesmerizing stars. Millions of them, lightyears away but it's like I can reach out and touch them. I lean against the control panel, taking care to avoid the buttons and switches.

This view... It's as if someone took the brightest light bulb in the world, painted in all the colours of Earth, turned it on, and was blinded by it.

"Ron-" I manage to say. "- this is unbelievable."

A huge grin creases his face as he stands up admiring the view himself.

"This is only the beginning. Honestly, no matter how many planets I visit, seeing Earth like this is different."

"Because it's home?"

He falls silent but I see his hand twitch at the comment.

"Wanna' better view?"

"W-- what do you mean by that?"

Ron crosses back towards the access hatch to the floor below. I follow, my steps hesitant. *I've trusted him this far, haven't I?* We climb back down to the bottom floor. He stands next to the entry door to the ship and grabs his Jericho Watch by the strap, pressing a latch where the buckle has been replaced. It falls into his hand.

"Hold out your wrist."

"Please don't throw me out the door. I don't want to die floating in space."

He grabs my wrist fitting the contraption in a tight lock.

"Don't be silly; I would never kick you out of my ship."

"What about the dying part?"

He smiles, reaching towards the door.

"Oh ya, that too!"

The word *"stop"* forms on my lips, but before I know it, the door is sliding open, revealing a thin blue barrier protecting us from the vacuum of space. A white noise fills the hanger around us. Looking back down at my body I gasp.

"What is this?!" The same barrier wraps around my entire body. Beyond my glasses, I see a light sapphire tint.

Ron chuckles, "These blue barriers are like space suits! They'll protect you in any environment!"

He moves quickly behind me, pushing his hands firmly against my shoulder blades. I scream bloody murder, performing a front flip through the door.

I'm going to die! I wave my arms around, trying to grab onto something, anything! All I can hear is Ron's laughter.

"Open your eyes!" he calls.

His calm voice seems to be coming from inside my bubble.

I guess I don't have any other choice!

I'm outside the ship, enveloped in space and all its dark beauty. It wraps me in its arms, its coruscating lights dancing within its velvet cloak. When the adrenaline flow slows and my heart returns to a subtle beat, I reach out, attempting to grab distant stars. My feet float in a semicircle, involuntarily looking at Ron and the ship. He's standing with his arms crossed in the safety of Eunoia. He disappears for a second and I experience a wave of fear. *This better not be a ploy to abandon my dead body in space!*

Eunoia makes a strange high-pitched whirr, a blue nylon cord appears from the underbelly of the ship. It shoots towards me, attaching itself to my suit. Ron's voice speaks reassuringly in my ear.

"This is a safety line attaching you to the ship!" I look down at the thin nylon thread, its twenty feet in length. *Looks flimsy to me, but I have to trust Ron.*

Using the momentum from a leg kick, I aim my head towards Earth, soaking in its beauty. That's when something catches my eye...a black dot, getting bigger, as if something is flying towards me.

"Uhm, Ron!"

That's when it hits me.

ANOTHER ALIEN TRIES TO EAT MY FACE

No, it literally hits me.

The incoming attacker rams against my suit, sending me into a spiral. My stomach does a 180 as I flip head-over-heels. The connector reaches the end of its length, recoiling like a bungee cord. I'm flung through the dark void of space feeling like Tarzan swinging on a vine. Except there are no trees or gorillas, and I'm screaming like a little girl.

Smashing into the underside of the ship, white sparks dance across my vision. Trying my best to piece together what just walloped me in the chest, the answer comes crawling across the underbelly of the ship, swinging it's twin tails in excitement.

Another one?! What am I some sort of Alien magnet?

The Spawn opens its mouth, aiming its fangs in my direction, scurrying towards me.

"Ron! Help!"

The ship trembles, my connector tugs, whatever my brother is trying to do, he'll be too late. *No! This is not the time to rely on Ron!!*

The Spawn lunges. With my feet against Eunoia's belly, I use the connector, twisting my body as I kick-off as hard as I can. Its momentum causes the Spawn to brush past my shoulder. My own momentum propels me to the end of my tether and the recoil swings me back towards the Euonia. Ron is talking urgently to Eunoia's A.I. and like a fish at the end of a hook, I'm reeled towards him.

"Get in! Quickly!" he shouts.

"What does it look like I'm doing? Having a tea party?!" I pass the barrier, my feet hitting the ship's floor as gravity returns to normal. Ron catches me.

"You're going to give me a heart attack!" I yell at him.
He grabs the Jericho Watch, deactivating my suit.

"A little adrenaline never killed anybody!" He grins.

I shake my head in disbelief. *I'm nearly killed and*

it amuses him? He slaps the watch on his wrist and then pulls out his gun, which immediately ripples with plasma energy up to the barrel.

"Hey man, it's not my fault Spawn like ya' so much!"

He presses a button and the door begins to slide closed. A shout rips through me.

"Look out!"

The monster has slithered through the crack in the closing door, head-butting Ron in the face. He's pinned against the nearest wall with the monster's paws crushing his chest. I hear his grunts over the rumble of the locking doors and the deactivating shields. Ron fires his gun into the monster's stomach. The bullet punches through the back of the Spawn, whizzing past my face. I backpedal, losing my balance. Although clearly hurt, the Spawn doesn't back down, rearing up on its hind legs, jaws snapping. Ron ducks, the Spawn sinks its teeth into a collection of tubing.

Barrel rolling, Ron aims, and fires. The blast misses, exploding against the wall in a shower of sparks. The Spawn kicks Ron in the face and he slams into my chest as the world flips upside down. I witness his gun skid underneath the ladder.

Ron and I roll. The Spawn shakes itself, flashing its wicked fangs. Something glints under a bench. A wrench. Adrenaline pumping, I clutch the cold metal in my hand, aim, and throw!

Clank... It strikes a furred ear, and then rebounds, dropping to the floor.

"ROAR!" Power shifts to the Spawn's haunches. I raise my arms, ready to be chewed up like a dog-toy. I see Ron's rising concern. He shoves me out of the way. Rolling once more, we stand side-by-side. Now unarmed, he pushes me behind him.

"Maybe, now is a bad time to tell you I left my good weapons in the car."

My eyes are drawn to the ladder.

"The locker.."

"What?"

I have no time to explain. The Spawn jumps at Ron. I squeeze out from behind him and rush to climb up the ladder. Behind me, the continued ruckus of their escalating battle continues. *I need to move fast!*

Jumping into the main deck, I rush for the weapons locker. *How the heck do I open this darn thing!?* EON's voice echoes throughout the ship.

"Access denied. Please use the retinal scanner."

A clanking-bang behind me startles me. I turn

around to see Ron clambering up the ladder. The Spawn's snarls send shivers down my spine.

"Break it open!!" Ron yells.

I ram my shoulder into the glass but it just cracks. *I need something to wrap around my hand.*

Ron's wardrobe? I rip it open, pulling out a sweater which I fashion around my hand.

"Take this!"

I punch the glass; it explodes. I turn back to grin at Ron and almost choke. He's on his back facing the Spawn's gigantic head. He kicks it in the teeth, making a satisfying crack. It snaps at his foot in response.

Light glints off metal in the locker. I clench my fist, gripping a random weapon with my sweaty hand and tossing it at Ron. My brother catches the now-visible blaster like a pro, aiming through the scope at the monster.

"Headshot sucker!"

BLAM! The Spawn's head splits. It howls before exploding into a ball of dark mist, evaporating completely.

I stand stiff as a statue, my laboured breathing cramping my chest. Ron glances my way. He raises an eyebrow.

"Two Spawn attacks in one day? You're a magnet for trouble."

"That's what I was thinking." I agree.

We are both breathing heavily from the attack and collapse gratefully onto one of the sofas. Ron deactivates his gun then turns to me, biting his lower lip.

"That was amazing work by the way. Looks like you were made for this kinda thing."

The ship falls quiet; he stares down at the floor and a dozen conflicting thoughts run through my mind as he watches me. *Is this the life I want?* I come to a quick decision.

"I agree."

He breaks out a big grin.

"Ya- exactly!"

Standing, he offers me his hand, hoisting me to my feet.

"So- when do I get to do that again?" I ask.

He snickers. "Maybe not too soon."

∆∆∆

"Ron, I'm sorry about the locker."

"Don't worry bro; I'll clean up the mess. It's happened before. Time to get you back home."

We clamber up to the flight deck and Ron instructs the AI. With Eunoia cloaked, we make our way down to the Big Red Slide park. The storm from earlier has passed. The sun begins to set as we land on the damp grass. Already, I miss the view from above. Ron turns to face me.

"Alright, here's the game plan."

"Yes, coach?"

He grins.

"I'll meet you here tomorrow morning. Pack like you're going out for a sleepover...some pj's and a change of boxers will do."

He crosses his arms in deep thought.

"Hm, some lined paper too. A binder, maybe your laptop? Do you have one of those?"

"I do."

Ron's nods, seemingly satisfied, but then his shoulders tense, his arms dropping.

"One last thing... if you happen to change your mind, tell me tomorrow morning. Take tonight to think about it."

I shake my head.

"I've made my decision Ron."

He nods and then places his hand on my shoulders. He looks down at me and I have never seen him look more serious

"I know ...I know...just, it's a whole new world, Finn. Being a Citadel member is hard work. We're going to be the only humans that they will have recruited. It will be up to us to represent our planet, in hopes of showing them what we're capable of. Don't agree to do this...just to bring me home. I mean it. You won't make it if you're doing this for me, or mom and dad."

He crosses his arms.

"It's gotta be about all of the earth too. They'll be counting on us, whether they know it or not."

He pauses for a moment, holding my eyes with his.

"Promise me you'll think about."

I nod.

"I will."

ΔΔΔ

My head is swimming with millions of thoughts as I make my way home. The first thing I do is doubt myself, *Am I brave enough to become a Cita-*

del member? Will I be smart enough? Can I become earth's hope to move on into a new age? Then the panic sets. *Ron will hate me if I abandon him. What if mom and dad find out the truth?*

Night envelops the cloudy sky. I shiver against the fall wind, wrapping my arms around my exposed skin. Even though Ron gave me new socks, my shoes are still wet, the fabric doing little to keep out the dampness.

Focusing on the city helps calm my thoughts. I stare at the overhanging trees; light posts guide my way down a silent street with secluded houses. Home comes into view in the distance. Dad's white Mercedes is parked in the driveway. *I thought he wasn't returning for another week?*

Remembering my fight with Chad, I grimace. If there's anybody I don't want to get in trouble with, it's my father. With mom, I can pass off her anger with a smile and an apology. No such thing with dad. I open my backpack, pulling out my cold house key, slipping it into the lock and opening the basement door. *Maybe they went to bed early?*

The shuffling from the living room overhead tells me different. I close the door, sliding my shoes off like a ninja, managing to tip-toe across the carpet into the downstairs hall before my father's assertive voice calls out,

"Finn Bates. Upstairs, now."

I turn back towards the stairs, climbing each step with growing anxiety. Mom and Dad are sitting on the long black leather couch. In front of them is a mahogany coffee table, littered with note-covered papers. Dad squints. His brown eyes are razor sharp behind his glasses. His short black hair is tousled. He's still wearing his work outfit, a clean black dress shirt tucked into a pair of dress pants with a gold belt. He stands. Mom stares at me, a thousand emotions racing across her face, which I cannot interpret. Moms' long black hair is tied in a ponytail. She's wearing her usual yellow sweater with blue jeans. Wrinkles have begun to form around her lips, grey hairs sprouting up like shrubs around her hairline.

Dad crosses his arms.

"What are you wearing?"

I glance down at the shirt Ron gave me.

"I went to the thrift shop today."

My voice wavers. Father shakes his head.

"Your principal, Mrs. Malkin, called just as I got home. Told me you got in a fight with some boy named Chad Brunestick?"

"He...was being a jerk dad. You don't understand..."

"Is he one of those bullies? I told you! They're bothering you because you make yourself a target."

"T- that's not true! Chad was talking about Ron again..." I stammer.

His name causes my pulse to quicken. *He's alive, Mom and Dad! He's on a ship, right now, at the Big Red Slide Park! Right- way to get myself locked up in the looney bin.*

Biting my tongue, I stare down at the floor.

"It won't happen again, I promise."

Dad snaps.

"No. It won't. Because you won't be going back to that school after Christmas break."

He makes it sound like a bad thing.

"Yes, sir'"

I clench my fists open, then closed. He walks around the end of the couch to stand in front of me face-to-face.

"You have something else on your mind? Say it."

My annoyance erupts.

"I'm surprised you're home is all! I didn't think you lived here anymore."

His eyebrows crease. Harsh wrinkles form around his nose and lips.

"I've been working a lot lately, Finn."

His face flushes.

"Unlike your mother, who enjoys staying at home crying with her head in a pillow."

To my surprise, Mom doesn't say anything. I look over, wanting her to fight back, but she remains still, brushing tears from her eyes.

"Don't say that about her," I say angrily.

Father grits his teeth, but despite the warning signs, I press on.

"It's not her fault, Ron is gone. It's not her fault that you only come home once every three months to ridicule us!"

Dad's calm facade shatters.

"Don't you dare speak to me like that! You two wouldn't have a roof over your head if it wasn't for me!"

I look back at the papers on the coffee table; my eyes dart down to the floor where a new travel bag is being packed.

"Looks like you're not even going to stay for dinner."

He grabs me by the hem of my shirt. My heels lift from the floor. My breath catches. Mom launches to her feet. Her voice is soft and mellow, but with a sharp edge.

"James, let him go. Finn is just stressed right now with all his studies. Graduating early is a lot of pressure. Right?"

Her voice calms him a little. Although my father has never been one to lay hands on me, my stomach won't stop twisting. He knits his hands together. That's when, for a brief moment, I see an ageing man before me, riddled with exhaustion. He unhands me. My wet socks slip as I stumble. Dad makes no move to assist me.

"I leave tomorrow morning to catch my flight to Alberta."

He walks back to the coffee table.

"And, yes, I won't be home for a few months. When I do come back, we can discuss your bursaries for University."

I nod. To say anymore is pointless. Neither of us is willing to apologize. My eyes turn to mother's and she gives a soft smile, nodding. *Guess it's time for me to leave.*

Overwhelmed, I go downstairs to my basement bedroom, opening the door then slamming it behind me. My backpack drops onto the floor. I sit on my bed with my face in my hands. The sound of another argument between my parents erupts. It makes me sick to my stomach. The bruising on my back, from when I slammed into Eunoia during the Spawn attack, changes my focus. My shoulders are stiff, too; rolling them, I attempt to massage the tender spots.

My room isn't big. There's a desk in the corner with my computer tower, my wardrobe and some posters of various quotes I moderately enjoy. Other than that, the room is blank. Devoid of personality. *I'm not going to be this person anymore.*

Through the ceiling, I hear Mother's desperate voice shout to father something along the lines of:

"Stay___what about Finn___if only! Please!"

This goes on for another few minutes. Meanwhile, I finish massaging my back, changing into a pair of sweatpants, and throwing my brother's shirt near my backpack. Dad's feet stomp out of the living room to their bedroom. Everything is silent.

Gritting my teeth, I roll my shoulders one last time. I open the closet which is full of all my old school memorabilia. What I'm searching for sits on top of an old science project. The water-proof duffle bag is old but has a lot of storage space. In the bag go extra clothes. My laptop sits on the bed. *Do I take it or not? Will the aliens have better computers?* In the end, I grab the thing, stuffing it in the bag along with the charger.

With Mom and Dad in their bedroom, I slip into my bathroom to grab a toothbrush. *Gotta make sure I smell good when meeting all the Aliens.*

Now that I am ready. I tuck myself in bed, attempting to sleep but my anxiousness is a bug that itches my brain, making me toss and turn. A haunting cry echoes from the kitchen. *Mom...*

Eventually, I fell asleep, wishing I was strong enough to go upstairs and hold her in my arms.

I FIND A TALKING BUG

I wake to the sound of my father slamming his bedroom door. I roll over in bed, staring at my door as his footsteps move over the hallway floor. The house falls silent before his car engine revs up, and he's gone.

Struggling and failing to doze off, I lie awake in the darkness of the cold, fall morning. It seems to be calling me. I accept the call, sitting up in bed, rubbing the sleep from my eyes. My sore feet are chilly against the hardwood floor. Getting dressed into a pair of grey jeans and a brown sweatshirt, I take my glasses and clean the lenses before propping them up on the bridge of my nose.

Opening my bedroom door, I creep into the downstairs hall, glancing out the window next to the boot room closet. It's still dark outside, stars speckling the dark sky and a lingering quarter-moon on the far horizon. Pulling out my cell phone from my back pocket, I glance at the time.

Six am, the sun should be up in an hour or two.

My hand gingerly grasps the door handle, attempting not to disturb mom. Stepping onto the sidewalk, I begin my walk to the park. Cars drive past, interrupting the tranquil silence. I plug in my earpieces to drown them out and listen to my favourite band. Strange to remember that I will miss their new releases so I make the most of this one as I walk. Thirty minutes later I arrive at the park. Gleaming frost lingers on the blades of grass.

Making my way down the hill, I attempt to locate Eunoia, extending my arm. Eventually, my palm rests against her cold underbelly. Forming a fist, I knock twice. Silence! I frown, trying again.

Knock, knock. I cross my arms.

Ron did say to meet up in the morning, right?

I take a step backwards, shaking my head in frustration. That's when Ron takes down her invisibility cloak, the side door slides open, allowing the ramp to descend towards me. Up in the shadows, Ron steps into the light, leaning against the framework, and yawns!

He's wearing a pink t-shirt and white pyjama pants decorated with sleepy elephants hugging fluffy pillows. His hair is a mess; his arms fall to his sides.
I hide my amused smile.

"I said in the morning dude! The sun ain't up yet."

"Well, the morning is subjective. I usually wake up at six."

Ron rubs his eyes, trying to push away black bags.

"Six? You're a monster."

He waves me onto the ship, and the ramp glides back into its housing. The door closes and locks behind me. We clamber up the ladder to the crew deck. The couch is covered by tossed-aside blankets and pillows. He has, however, managed to clean up the broken glass from the locker that I smashed open yesterday. I set my bag on the couch and sit beside it.

Ron fixes his messy hair by combing his hand through the thick locks. His weapons still lie where they fell. The armory access panel is arcing, shooting sparks into the air. He ignores it and heads for the flight deck.

"Back in a moment. Need to restore the cloaking."

Soon, he's back on the crew deck

"I guess it's a good thing you woke me up. Time is gonna get all wonky when we reach Altair."

"How big of a time difference are we talking about?"

"The days on Altair are shorter."

He rummages around on the dirty floor, locating his soiled outfit from yesterday. He starts to change. I stare out the window.

"One day on Altair is a quarter day here on Earth. You could spend a night, morning n' evening at HQ, it would only be round' 5 pm here on Earth."

Now that he's fully dressed, we head up again to the flight deck where he flops into the pilot's seat.

"Godsonion Ulmu will be impressed; I'm back early."

"Who or what is a Godsonion Ulmu?"

"Each Citadel outpost has a head honcho who calls the shots. Ours is Godsonion Ulmu. Trust me, he may look intimidating, but he's a big softy."

I'll believe that when I meet him.

Ron activates EON and instructs "her" to set coordinates for Altair.

EON's seductive voice announces.

"Altair Destination set. System checks in progress. Departure at T-Minus ten minutes."

He gestures me over to take the co-pilot's seat.

"Belt yourself in." he instructs me.

I do as he says.

"So, you ready?"

"Absolutely."

"Alright!"

EON's count-down begins.

"Five, four, three, two, one..."

We are swept into the sky. I am amazed again at the rate at which we hurtle through the cloud layer, and the darkness of dawn is replaced with the soft light of distant stars.

"Beginning the hyperdrive sequence."

It's just like in the movies. Eunoia appears to be sucked into an inverted hole of darkness; and then we flash past white lines and violet hues. I gaze, fascinated by the flashing, vibrating patterns visible through the viewport until EON's voice announces:

"Leaving Hyper-space in 30 seconds".

Once again, there is no real sensation. One moment the light patterns revert to inky blackness and moments later, constellations appear outside, but not the familiar ones, like The Plough, or Orion's Belt. These patterns are noticeably different.

"Entering Altair Perimeter Control Zone."

Leaning back in my chair, I lay eyes on the mind-blowing Altair HQ. Ron claps his hands spreading his arms wide.

"Altair, meet Finn. Finn meet Altair!"

He waits for me to be amazed. I am. I had imagined Altair to be on a planet, but oh how wrong I was!

The Citadel outpost of Altair *is* a planet, resembling a floating hamster ball.

"Holy cow," I gasp. "It's the size of Pluto!"

"You're close." Ron nods. "We both have a diameter of just around 1,500 miles."

"You're joking!" I say in disbelief.

"You'll find out." he tells me.

As we get closer, I can see that the outer shell is a leaden grey and so huge that, close-up, its surface appears flat. At intervals, the exterior is pierced by sections that look as though they are made of a glass-like material.

"It's...the Death Star."

"I've never heard it called that before." Ron laughs.

EON pings. *"Docking Control is requesting ID"*

"Put them on speaker" Ron replies

"Approaching vessel, Ship ID" a loud, gruff voice demands,

"Hey!" Ron calls. "Clubb, It's Ron. I'm glad to hear you on radio duty."

The voice on the other end maintains its official tone.

"That's Phender Clubb to you. These calls are recorded so try to be professional for once." he says, but he can't keep the amusement out of his voice.

"Eunoia K98, ID 492846. I brought a friend!" Ron announces.

I smile at him.

"So, you accomplished your recruitment mission?" Clubb responds, "You know, some of the others won't be too happy about that."

Ron's eyes widen. He gives me an awkward sideways glance.

"Hey, let's not talk like that."

I give a concerned frown. *It looks as though I'm not going to be as welcomed as I had imagined. Could that be because I'm human? Ron did warn me about it...*

"Clear for Landing Bay 12 Level 452. Godsonion

Ulmu will greet you."

"Roger that. Out."

The intercom goes dead.

"So...do humans have a bad rep?" I ask.

Ron closes his eyes, taking in a deep breath.

"Well, we aren't known as the smartest species."

We leave it at that. I assume by the way his face tightens, he doesn't want to bother me with harsh realities so soon. *I'm prepared. I'll be strong.*

"There is one thing I didn't warn you about."

Ron tells me.

"Because there are already over 30 species manning Altair, it would be impossible to provide them with their home atmosphere so, when we arrive, the first thing that will happen is we'll be led into a sealed medical chamber that's been set to Earth normal..for you to receive a Rhinometer."

"Which is what?" I ask nervously.

"Think of it as acting like a very advanced pacemaker but instead of being connected to your heart, it is connected to your lungs and nasal cavities!"

"Why do I need a Rhinometer...?

"Well, the atmosphere of most planets is made up of a mixture of different gasses, so the Rhinometer analyses the mixture and automatically adjusts your metabolism to compensate so that all species on Altair can breathe the ship's atmosphere."

"How...?" I start

"Don't ask. I dunno! Right! Down we go."

Eunoia sails towards Altair and, as we get closer, I can make out multiple see-through plasma shields that allow ships into the numerous landing bays. It reminds me of filing cabinets, and we are files about to be neatly tucked into place.

Ron keeps his hands lightly on the yoke, ready for any last-minute manual adjustments but EON's A.I. lands us gently as a feather.

We have landed on a metal platform. Ron throws some switches on the overhead control panel. Lights go from green to red and then off as Eunoia closes down. He rises to his feet, scooping up my bag. He throws it at me, and it tumbles into my outstretched arms.

"Just stick with me, you'll be fine."

Doing as he says, we exit the ship via the airlock. As the outer door opens, I find myself walking along an airtight tunnel. For some reason, I seem to be having difficulty adjusting my step. Ron glances at me and a broad grin spreads across his face.

"I wondered how long it would take you to notice. Gravity is about 70 per-cent of Earth's, so be careful making physical movements. Don't worry. You'll soon get used to it. It makes lifting things easier."

I suddenly realise that my pack feels lighter. *I can get used to this!*

Ron leads the way and at the end of the hall is an open steel door. As soon as we enter the "New Arrivals Medical Suite", the steel door closes and seals. There is a floating platform-like-bed that appears to be adjustable for both width and length.

Ron follows my gaze.

"Well, not all recruits are our size." he says.

"I guess, but this room seems surprisingly bare for a medical facility."

"Ya, but it only does one thing...installing Rhinometers. The main medical floors are higher up."

At that moment, what I would call a robot detaches itself from a wall and hovers over to us. It glides on two wheels and comes up to my hip in height.

"Greetings, human."

I almost laugh because its voice sounds like CP30 from "Star Wars".

"Please take off your shirt and lie down on the bed. This procedure will take 15 of your Earth minutes and you will feel nothing."

Not altogether reassured, I do as I'm told. The robot moves to one side of me and I feel a slight jab in my thigh.

"Okay," Ron says. "Put on your shirt and let's go."

"But what about the implant?" I ask.

"It's done." he says.

I get off the bed and see that the robot is now re-attached to the wall. I look down at my chest and see a six-inch incision scar that is fading even as I watch. *It seems that we have a lot to learn back home!*

Ron and I exit the medical suite through a door on the opposite side from the entrance and emerge into Altair's interior. The smell of metal mixed with sea salt hits me but it's a reassurance to realise that I can breathe this air. I gawk in awe at my surroundings.

The loading bay is noisy. I tune into the clanging

of ship parts being replaced. In a side-bay, engines under test whine like banshees. As far as the eye can see are solid walls made from sheets of an unfamiliar metal, doors with panels, and flashing buttons.

That's when I spot my first alien, a small fish-like being the height of a German Shepherd. Its ultramarine scales blend into its uniform. It is wearing a Prussian Blue T-shirt made from strange material. It has a black band at the bottom, and a white hip sash tied in a fancy knot. In its webbed hands, it holds a tablet fitted with a laser pen.

Another alien strolls past my right-hand side. It's a humanoid, with feathered hair; its face is tipped with a small yellow beak. It has four arms, and two digitigrade shaped legs. It is speaking a language into its Jericho Watch. At least, I assume it's a language but the sounds it makes are unintelligible to me.

Looking over at Ron, I wonder if I'm dreaming. He waves his hand in front of my face. I blink, allowing the reality of it all to process. He laughs.

"Just make sure not to stare for too long."

Nodding, a childlike grin erupts on my face.

"I'll try."

However, curiosity persuades me to look back. *They are so cool!* Around us, more aliens appear, of all different shapes and sizes. Some have rainbow-coloured skin; others look like animals. Clearly, alien worlds breed an infinite number of life-forms. A chuckle lingers on my lips, *It's so crazy, that we humans have no idea beings like this exist!*

On the other side of the bay, a door opens with a swoosh. Through the entryway comes an alien walking with grace and dignity, much like the King of England. This new individual strongly resembles an over-grown insect; his body is humanoid with tiny brown scales that spread up his arms and chin. He has an oval face, two large black eyes, and a small square mouth. He has a short scut. His uniform is eye-catching. It looks to be made of satin threads in shades of purple and blue. Frills fall past the elbows. There is a definite twinkle in his eyes.

"Ron, I'm glad you made it back."

His voice is high-pitched, keen, yet calm and pacifying.

Ron gives a casual nod, looking at me.

"This is him."

The alien looks down at me, and I have the strangest feeling that I sense admiration in his gaze.

"Ah, Finn Bates. I'm so happy that you accepted our request. This is no small task you plan on undertaking."

A reply forms on my lips, but timidness stops me.

"It's alright; I know it is a lot to take in at first. I am Godsonion Ulmu the ranking officer on Altair."

"Uh, my name is Finn. Nice to meet you, sir."

Ulmu's scut twitches.

"Why don't we all go to my office? It will be more comfortable there."

He turns in one swift motion and moves off extremely quickly. Ron is already pursuing him. I flip my pack, as I normally would, and it flies into the air.

Fortunately, I am holding one of the straps and I restrain it before slipping it onto my shoulder. *Lesson one about lower gravity, don't throw things at full strength!*

By this time, Ron and Ulmu are some way ahead but I learn lesson number two by speed-walking and catching up with them easily.

We exit the Landing Deck at one end into a wide corridor and face a long bank of elevators.

"Wow!" I exclaim, staring along the bank. "That's a whole heap of elevators!"

"Indeed it is-" Ulmu says "-but with over 500

levels and nearly 100,00 staff, you could wait a week for one when we are busy. Even now, service can be a little slow."

However, as he finishes speaking, one arrives and we step in. As the doors close, my eyes are drawn to the see-through floor. A dark shaft drops away below us into blackness. Godsonion Ulmu sees me staring down.

"We are twenty levels above the Hotherium fission core which provides the power for Altair." Godsonion Ulmu explains. "More precisely, we are above the radiation containment shielding which surrounds it. At the lowest level of the core is where our gravity control system operates."

"Amazing..."

"Level One." Ulmu orders to the elevators A.I.

"*Level One*" a disembodied voice repeats.

The elevator starts to rise and accelerates until the view becomes a grey blur. I can't keep the look of surprise off my face.

"Ah, yes!" Ulmu says. "The elevators are all controlled by gravitics, rather like the ship that brought you here. To cover so many levels, they have to be capable of moving us very quickly. If they could not ensure a smooth start and finish, you would hit the roof of the car as it dropped down, and be crushed into the floor as it stopped."

"That's...scary. I hadn't thought of that" I respond.

"My Office and quarters form Level One, at the peak of Altair. They overlook the Oprea Galaxy." Ulmu says.

I look over at my new Godsonion.

"What else is in the Oprea Galaxy?"

"You are an inquisitive individual; you'll do well here, Finn," he smiles. "Only Altair HQ, and the native planet of Montai' are in this galaxy. The Citadel attempts to remain untraceable by placing Outposts in distant galaxies..."

Ron shrugs.

"Not that Spawn, Raiders, or this Odium punk would be bold enough to attack us. We'd blow em' to smithereens."

"Mighty confident, as per usual, Bates."

Ron gives a smile.

Our elevator slows to a smooth halt and the doors open onto a beautiful blue hallway, beneath a concrete archway. Ulmu leads us into his large, comfortable-looking office beyond. The walls are silver and totally undecorated. A sapphire carpet is soft under my shoes.

A white desk is situated next to a large window. I stare at the vastness of space beyond. *What a fantastic view!*

Ron plops into the nearest visitor's chair. It squeaks. I follow suit. The cushion is remarkably soft. Ulmu's chair is white. He sits.

I can't tear my gaze away from the vastness of space as seen through the large window behind his desk.

"This is really amazing," I say in awe.

"It is extraordinary isn't it?" he says.

Ulmu points to a door in the far wall.

"I am privileged to have extensive luxurious living quarters behind that door over there. Even after all the time I have spent here, I am still in awe of the view. I am also fortunate that most of my duties can be conducted from this office. Indeed, the hardest part of this job is to leave this office but… now, Finn, I'll start off as I would for any new recruit."

He folds his three long fingers together resting them under his chin. A soft smile lingers on his lips.

"We, at the Citadel, have a ranking system, much like Earth's military. On acceptance, one starts at the bottom as a Fledgil, upgrading to Aster Bronze when you pass the upgrade exam. In your case, that is where you will start ...studying to become an Aster Bronze. Then comes Aster Gold and Aver Bronze First Class; finally Aver Gold. Then there are specialty groups such as Engineers, Researchers, Medicos, and so on. But you need not bother yourself with them for the time being."

He pauses to lean back in his chair.

"Upgrading is accomplished by attending classes. We have courses you are obligated to take. Others that you may add to your agenda as you see fit. Your first challenge will be to pass the acceptance exam to become an Aster Bronze."

I didn't know I was going to be loaded with homework...I guess they wouldn't just throw me out into space without any training.

"You will have your own quarters here on Altair, and you may come and go as you wish. With the assistance of a higher-up, you may even be permitted to join a low ranked mission, depending on how you progress."

The excitement in my face fades.

"So, I won't be going on missions with Ron?"

Ulmu pauses and laughs. It's a high pitched, jovial sound.

"Certainly not as a Fledgil. Pass your upgrade exam and become an Aster Bronze, and it may be possible if the mission is classed as low-ranked."

Ron butts into the conversation. He points at his chest with his thumb.

"Shoulda told ya,' I'm an Aver Bronze bro, on my way to becoming an Aver Gold."

Ulmu cuts him off.

"Not with that level of arrogance, you're not!"

They banter, as a family would. Despite being told that humans aren't welcome, Ulmu and Ron's relationship gives me hope that acceptance is possible.

"Ron's not going to be your mentor yet, Finn. And I should tell you that if you can't pass the Entrance Exams, both mental and physical, your memory will be wiped, and you will be sent back to Earth."

...WHAT!!??

Ron leans in, patting me on the back.

"Don't worry! You'll do fine! You're a smart kid. Besides, you'll have a whole week to study."

Ulmu shakes his head.

"Two days actually."

Here it comes. My heart is beating a mile a minute. If I keep up this level of stress, I'll be dead before I can take any exam. My voice trembles.

"Do I have some reference works to study?"

Ulmu opens his drawer and takes out a thick book.

"Of course, Finn. This contains everything you'll need for your exam.

He offers the book to me and I take it from his hand. It weighs about 2 kilos. *Is he kidding? I have to master this in just two days? I might just as well start planning for the trip back to Earth!* Ulmu doesn't seem to consider the impossibility of this challenge as he continues his introduction address.

"Once you become Aster Bronze, you will acquire all your equipment, including our treasured Jericho Watch. I assume your brother has shown you his?"

I nod.

"Good. Don't fret. Ron made you pack your belongings for a reason. Time moves differently on Altair."

He opens another drawer.

"One last thing..."

He pulls out a black T-shirt with the word "Fledgil" printed on the back, then a small earpiece connected to a sleek, silver oblong that looks as though it should clip onto a belt. I take them from his hands.

Ulmu gestures to the piece of equipment.

"That is a universal translator. All Citadel sanctioned planets are given translators to ensure seamless communication. Make sure to use it immediately, and wear that shirt, so that other ranks don't get the wrong idea."

Ulmu's eyes are alight with amusement. His looks as though he is turning something over in his mind. I stare at him, letting my own determined gaze meet his own.

"I wish you the best of luck, Finn Bates. I'm sure you will find many ways to surprise us."

A DRAGON KARATE KICKS MY FACE

Ulmu dismisses us and we make our way to one of the elevators. As we walk, I position the translator's earpiece in my ear. It fits comfortably. I press the center button on the control box and a quick pinging sounds in my ears to indicate that it is active.

Out of earshot of his boss, Ron lights up with a bubbly conversation.

"So, Altair has six hundred plus floors-"

We stand in front of an elevator.

"-the elevators respond to voice command. They recognize the floor number of the destination or its name. For example, you could say either "452" or "Launch Bay 2B" and it will take you there. That's useful if you know where you want to go but not the level that it is on."

An elevator arrives and we get in.

"Level nine." Ron says.

"*Level nine.*" The voice responds.

The doors open at Level Nine onto a corridor along which a number of assorted uniformed aliens are moving around. They look at Ron and I, some with curiosity while a couple of alien faces register what I can only interpret as distaste.

As we move along the corridor, I see that there are a large number of holographic "pictures" identifying the various species resident, but Ron isn't represented. We reach a door with a retinal scanner. Below the scanner is a plaque that reads "915". Ron places his eye against the scanner and the door clicks open. He steps inside and I follow.

I'll be honest. I don't know what I was expecting from my big brother's quarters, but it wasn't this.

Some things never change, and Ron's military training has not made him any tidier. His room is the size of a standard hotel room, and it's a mess. The bathroom is on my left, a sizeable closet is on my right. The bathroom smells like lemony-bleach and the shower stall is a large glass pillar with a tiled floor and three showerheads. Ron's bed juts out of the wall, floating without legs. It has a white mattress with a black blanket and soiled pillows; A white canopy overhangs it.

There is a viewport on the far wall, but it is covered, masking whatever is beyond.

Gazing up at the ceiling, I see the large circular light which is giving his bedroom a soft white glow. Schoolwork is scattered about like confetti; a half-empty coffee cup filled with a mysterious brown liquid has left a circular stain on a page of a notebook which lies half-open on the floor. Leaning over, I frown at the thin layer of mold forming on the liquid's surface.

"Sorry bout' the mess," he says. "I was studying before I left."

While his back is turned, I scoop the coffee mug from the floor to his desk.

"Drop your stuff off here."

He pats his mattress. I toss my backpack towards it. It sails over the bed and lands on the floor on the other side. *Lesson number three about lower gravity.* I go and retrieve it, placing it firmly on the bed, trying not to pay attention to Ron's laughter.

I find a chair to sit in.

"You were telling me about Altair's layout." I say.

Ron continues to explain the layout.

"Right! Well, Military Quarters are on the second to twenty-fourth floors, right above the main hall. Higher ranking officers like me are on the ninth. As a new recruit, you will be on the twenty-fourth floor."

He puffs out his chest. *It looks like his initial embarrassment has worn off.*

"How many people live here?"

"Hm- round' ninety-seven thousand."

"How many?" I gasp.

"Only around ninety-seven thousand, but you've got to remember that we're actually the smallest Citadel Outpost, n' the newest. Even then, that's barely enough for the size of Altair."

My jaw drops.

"Ninety-seven thousand! Holy crap!"

"You bet." Ron explains. "As you know, the top floor is Ulmu's suite. Then you've got probably 50 floors for administrators. Some are concerned with everything that affects Altair itself and each of the 33 species is represented in that group. Their duties run from intelligence gathering to waste disposal and recycling, with everything in between.

Then each of the species we have here so far, has

dozens of administrators to look after the affairs unique to that species. Each species has ten to a dozen levels of accommodations and services required by that species.

Add in that there are the numbers of medical staff with specialist groups of physicians for each species, since they all have different internal organs and metabolisms. On top of that we have the guest astrophysicists, the maintenance staff, the house-keeping crews, and the large kitchen crews needed to create a wide variety of native foods. Most importantly are the military staff. It all adds up."

I am staggered by the numbers but, when he analyses it, it makes sense.

If Altair is the smallest outpost, my mind can't imagine the size of the bigger ones!

Ron interrupts my wandering thoughts with practical matters.

"I'll clear the floor n' grab ya' a sleeping bag." He grins. "But before that, how about you meet my best friend? She's a real firecracker."

"Sure", I say.

So, we go back into the hall and the door closes behind us. More students come and go, possibly from class. I pass a tiny dog-person wearing pyjamas. An elevator door opens and I see that most of the space is taken up by two large students with leather skin, bulbous heads and short, thick tails. We squeeze ourselves in and I'm forced to squish up against Ron's shoulder.

"Two-Six-Two" Ron says.

We ride down in silence, stopping once at their floor where Ron and I had to get out into the corridor to let them off. We get back in and the door slides silently closed. We resume our descent.

"What kind of species were they?"

"Mecek's. Real mean folk! Don't like anybody but themselves."

He pauses for dramatic effect.

"Also, Mecek's have acid glands that shoot venom out of their mouths, so don't pick a fight with em"

The elevator stops at Level 262 and the door opens.

We walk the length of the corridor and reach a dead-end. Frowning, I cross my arms.

"Does your friend live in the wall?"

He laughs.

"No, look down."

I do so and see a brass plate with an iron handle

set in the floor. Ron reaches down and pulls the door open, allowing a rush of warm air to hit me in the face. It smells of wood-smoke and copper. I see a shaft with a ladder clamped to the wall.

Ron lowers himself in and begins climbing down. I follow. The glow from above provides some dim illumination.

"She's in here."

He jumps off the last couple of steps and lands with a light thud. I make my way down a little more cautiously and find myself in a workshop, filled with a mind-blowing cluster of futuristic equipment and tools. Large red neon poles pulsing with energy are held against the metal rafter with heavy steel
clamps. What look like fighter craft are stationed above us on silver ramps. On the other side of the room, I see a ship hovering with a beam of energy causing the air to shimmer below it.

Looking down at my feet, I stare at a screwdriver that is the size of my arm. Everything that I can identify is twice the size of its earthly counterpart and there are many items that are completely alien. Even the roof spans slightly over 20 feet. To my left, an old school furnace, fitted with a metal plate on the inside, sends sparks into the warm air. Ron is looking around this vast area.

"Miv?"

Thump!

Ron crosses his arms.

"You don't wanna congratulate me on a mission well done?"

I scan the multiple metal contraptions and railings before spotting a monstrous lizard-like tail higher up, on a platform.

"Woah!"

Unnerved, I jump backwards but Ron is smiling up at the figure. The tail flicks, grating against the metal surface as it moves. A huge, scaly, clawed hand appears. Next comes an enormous head. It is like nothing I have ever seen before but it closely resembles my childhood images of a dragon. Seeing the broad grin on Ron's face, I figure that this must be Miv.

She – well I assume that it is a "she" - has dark-red scales and when her eyes flick open, they reveal yellowish-crimson irises against black. She looks down at me, huffing black smoke from her two nostrils. Razor-sharp teeth catch the light from the open fire. She has no wings. Instead, she has two arms fitted with tool belts and holsters.

"This must be your little brother. Greetings, Finn Bates"

She jumps, slamming onto the ground. Her tail

trails behind her. A growl rumbles from her chest before she speaks.

"I'm glad to see Ron will have assistance on his mission to finally go home"

Miv is wearing a scorched white shirt underneath a leather blacksmith's apron and a pair of loose pants rolled up to her knees. Her feet are bare, she also doesn't seem to notice the oil-stains on her ebony scales.

"He didn't take much convincing either. Just one or two bouts with a' spawn, n' he's battle-ready." Ron tells her.

Miv's tail curls up against her feet and she fixes her shirt. I can't stop staring up at her like I'm prey about to be eaten whole. She is, I would guess, about seven and a half feet tall.

"I see you are in shock, young Finn! Don't worry. That is a very normal reaction. I am the only Drakkinion on Altair. Many avoid me."

Ron walks up nudging her on the arm.

"Their loss! Now all your cool gear is all mine."

I think that the next sound she makes is her version of a laugh.

"Hm, if you promise not to tattle on me."

Miv nudges him in the chest with one of her

elongated claws. He stumbles, trying not to fall butt-first.

Miv turns her head to look at me.

"I'll explain. I'm an Engineer and I've created some unique gadgets. I can mod and create almost any tool, if given enough spare parts and time."

Miv looks back at my brother.

"So, you want something special for Finn, I assume?"

Smoke cascades from her nostrils as if heated by an internal fire. Ron nods.

"See, Finn's gotta' bit of a disadvantage. He's got two days before his exams. All the other lucky students get to study for months."

The fact sits like a rock in my stomach. Miv's tail twitches, she sits up straight.

"Yes, indeed. How unfair!"

She looks genuinely perturbed.

"Come"

She turns around.

"I have the perfect device to assist with your current predicament."

She leads us past the fighters into a back room.

A black metal box is lying crooked against the wall She gives it a tug and it bangs onto the floor. Opening it with one claw, she picks up a tiny chip, gesturing towards us. It looks like an ant in her oversized palm.

"This is my one of a kind 'Move Memorizer." she says.

"Move...Memorizer?" I say, puzzled. "What does it do?"

"It's what you earthlings might call an "aide-memoire'. You attach this chip to the back of your ear. When you are ready, click this little button once."

She points to a small blue button on one edge of the device.

"From what Ron tells me, you will be studying tactics. As you learn about attack maneuvers, the Move Memorizer will allow you to absorb and copy them exactly."

Miv ponders for a moment.

"For example, suppose you are in a battle with an individual who knows an advanced fighting style. Simply press this chip. Instantly, you will know their fighting style yourself."

Ron's eyes go wide.

"I'll take that one!" he says. "I never did have time

to learn karate-"

Miv slams her other hand over the chip, pulling away from him.

"No way!" she scolds him. "This is for Finn. I assume he has no battle training. Correct?"

I give a sheepish nod.

"The Move Memorizer is not Citadel sanctioned equipment; try to be discreet with it, ok?"

Opening my palm, she gingerly gives me the gadget. The device has a white face, and the back is blue and green. The tiny blue button is set on one edge.

"Why not try it? Place the white material on your skin."

I gently press the contraption behind my ear where it clicks into place.

"This is a prototype, so it can only memorize movement for ten-second intervals."

She grins.

"Also..."

I feel a sudden zap! A small electric shock races from the side of my skull to my eyes.

"...the connection programming between the chip and your eyes isn't fully refined, so it hurts a little when you first use it."

"Why would he want something that doesn't work?" Ron scoffs.

"It does work," she snaps at him. "The pain is worth it ...in his case."

"I- it's not that bad," I tell Ron.

"You see!" Miv says triumphantly. "How about a demonstration. I'll perform a mock attack Against Ron.

"So, I just have to look at you?"

"Directly, that's right. Now press the small black button."

She takes a step back, leaning against the wall. I trigger the contraption and the electric current I felt in short bursts turns into a slight rumble. My eyes widen as a light blue hue coats my cornea, lighting up Miv's form.

With her large tail, Miv makes a sweeping motion like a bat aiming for a baseball.

The force behind the blow sweeps past my face, the wind making me stumble onto my heels. Her tail curls into a resting position as she finishes the attack on all fours. Blinking twice, the hue disappears.

Zap! A tingle ripples through me as my left foot

automatically shifts into an arch.

"Allow your mind to copy the move." Miv instructs me. "Your body will follow."

Alright. Body... move! My other leg bends, I'm sent into an involuntary sweeping motion. Every muscle in my body tenses; my heart races with excitement.

"Woah!"

I'm astounded as my foot swings through the air, almost taking out Ron. I finish with my arms raised and fists closed, both feet on the ground, my balance perfect.

"Nice, dude!" Ron says. "That was a full-on karate kick!"

Zap!

"Augh!"

I rip off the chip, leaving a sticky residue behind. I glare at the memorizer in my hand.

"At the moment, the memorizer should only be used for short periods. It won't kill you although, as long as it is on, it will become progressively more painful. I'm working on a new model that will eliminate that problem. I'll let you know as soon as I have worked out the revised circuitry. It is in my nature to help my friends."

Looking up at her, I smile.

"Thank you, Miv; I appreciate this."

She nods.

"I wish you nothing but the best in your endeavors, Finn. It would benefit us greatly to have somebody like you on our side."

△△△

Ron and I climb back up the ladder to the corridor.

"That's enough of the serious stuff." He says. "Come on.

He leads the way back to the elevators and takes us to Level 31. As we walk together down the corridor, I hear the sound of laughter coming from one of the rooms. The pinging of a pin-ball machine confuses me. We pass the open door and I stop because I am fascinated to see strings of rainbow lights festooning the ceiling. They are interspersed by what look like the old-world neon lights. These are cycling through many colours but so subtly that it takes me a moment to recognize the changes. Shadows dance across the floor where a small group of assorted aliens are playing a game that completely mystifies me.

"This is weird! What are all these rooms for?"

My head spins as I hear the percussive sound of gunshots, but with an epic sound of action music, coming from another room across the corridor.

"This floor is the best, hands down."

He lifts three fingers then one.

"Thirty-one! It's the arcade, with games rooms, home theatre, library, sauna... you name it!"

What kind of army headquarters is this!? It's starting to sound like an all-inclusive vacation resort.

"Why do you have rooms like that?"

"Many of the staff spend their lives on Altair ... administration, maintenance, medical; it's their home. And there are also people like me. When we aren't on missions, we can come down here to unwind."

He notes.

"It's not like earth where you can travel to Europe or Hawaii for vacation. The Citadel does whatever it can to make their outposts as welcoming n' fun as possible. What would you like to see next?" Ron asks. "The swimming pool? The Library?

"Not now. Let's go back to your quarters." I tell him. "I need to study. If I don't pass these tests, I won't become an Aster, and I can't help you come home."

'Ya, I guess so." he nods "But there is one thing you need to see first"

We go back to the elevators which takes us to the twenty-fifth floor.

"Ulmu may have a great view of space, but we got something pretty fancy on this level too."

The elevator doors open up into a large lobby with several tall windows on all the walls overlooking the vastness of space. In the center is a gigantic Kraken statue, the tentacles swooping out and curling through the air. An alien with blue fur and one yellow eye sits on the edge of the concrete base with a holographic laptop. The Kraken fountain has two pools of knee-deep water, decorated with bright green lily pads and rainbow fish. Petite brown chairs paired with circular tables skirt them. I hear the sound of tumbling water. It is coming from a mini waterfall.

"Ron, this is...beautiful."

He smiles, looking to take it as a personal compliment.

"This is Altair's main hall." he says.

I am curious about the fountain.

"I've been meaning to ask you. Why's everything

water and fish-themed?"

"Let's get back to my quarters and I'll tell ya over some coffee, but being on the twenty-fourth floor, you're going to be looking down on this. Pretty neat, eh?"

"Sure sounds like it." I say.

We go back to his quarters and I settle down, coffee in hand.

"Now-"

Ron begins.

"-remember I told you there are five Citadel Outposts?" We are Altair; our sigil is the Kraken. Next is Vusta, the Lightning Bolt, Etis, of Nature, Jacriea, the Arrow and Othinda, the Sword. Originally these were just names, but over hundreds of years, the students took it upon themselves to give each of the HQ's a personality. You'll want to remember these as they'll likely be part of the acceptance exam."

"Im on it!" I tell him, sitting cross-legged on the floor and readying my pencils and pens, getting to work.

While I get down to studying, Ron starts to clean. He makes the bed, picks up his papers, throws out the mouldy coffee, and pulls out a sleeping bag from the spare closet.

Meanwhile, the first thing I read is a fun introductory paragraph...

"Hello, new Fledgil! Thank you for your interest in becoming a Citadel member. We want to make sure you are equipped with the knowledge to pass your exams and join our ranks. In this volume, you will find questions and answers, star charts, and other valuable information. Good luck, Fledgil."

"How come this is written in English?" I ask.

"Ulmu translated n' prepared it for ya. Want more coffee?"

"Yes, please." I answer while returning to my notes. "I have a feeling I won't be sleeping tonight anyway."

The distant hum of conversation in the main hall is a welcome white noise. When Ron returns with my coffee, we lapse into a comfortable silence. He pulls out a small square tablet with a stylus, beginning to scribble down his own work. The gentle 'tip' and 'tap' of the plastic against the bright screen comforts me. All my worries dissipate, allowing me to read with a clear mind.

"One of the most important things about being a Fledgil is knowing which six major galaxies Altair, protects."

I continue reading but, after a while, it all starts

to blur into gibberish. Scratching my head, I wipe my glasses, thinking, perhaps, the lenses are smudged. No luck. I feel Ron's eyes on me.

"Ya know, I am here to help," he says.

My tongue catches. *I've been studying for two hours now and I haven't talked to Ron once.* I sigh.

"I'm sorry, I'm an idiot. I'm used to studying alone. To tell the truth, I'm having trouble with this first chapter."

He takes the book, looking at it with a smile. As he reads, I drink my coffee, which has already needed to be refilled twice.

"The galaxies are sorted in alphabetical order," he begins. "So, we at Altair protect Galaxies K through P."

Another sip of my coffee.

"Huh?"

He thinks for a moment.

"This will be easier if I tell you how we map out the galaxies."

He pauses, working out how to best explain. He holds up a finger.

"On a Citadel Sanctioned map, if you were to try and find Altair, our coordinates would be written as K-A-2000."

He wiggles his finger as I furiously scribble notes that I hope to be able to read later.

"The 'K' is the galaxy."

He raises his next finger.

"The 'A' is the subsection of the said galaxy."

He raises his third finger.

"The '2000' is the planet."

He sees that I'm starting to understand. He drops his hand, giving one more example.

"My first ever mission was on a planet called Ra'lal'. The coordinates were M-C-2250. Get it?"

I nod vigorously.

"Got it. So, we protect galaxies K-P. What about the others?"

He crosses his arms thinking for a minute.

"Jacriea is A-J. Othinda is Q-S, Vusta, T-V, and Etis guards W-Z."

"Now this chapter is starting to make sense. Thanks, Ron."

He beams at having been able to help his "smarter" brother.

Taking my book, I go back to work, asking Ron random questions. Eventually, the sound of chit chatter outside dies into complete silence. The main hall dims, the music of the water fountain echoes. Finally, Ron stands up.

"Finn, I'm going to go to bed now, kay?'"

The room is silent.

"Eh Finn?"

"Huh?"

I look up from my papers, and it dawns on me what he just said.

"Oh, Okay. 'Night."

I look back down at the paragraphs that are swimming around in my brain. Ron gets up and slides into his bed. Now, the only noise is my stylus on paper. I'm unaware of how much time has passed. Blinking, I rub my eyes.

Ron is sprawled out like a starfish, fresh drool staining his fluffy pillow.

"Snore!"

I stifle a laugh. With a deep breath, I let my eyes close, falling backwards onto my sleeping bag, reaching out to fix my pillow, my eyes shut. I'm out like a light.

I MEET THE NEW CHAD BRUNESTICK

Scritch, scritch...scritch.

It sounds like somebody fishing through a haystack. Opening my eyes, I find myself staring up at the roof. I'm still fully clothed, with my reference papers covering my feet like a throw blanket.

Taking off my glasses, I roll over on my side. Within the blurry mess, Ron's figure steps out of the bathroom smiling.

"Waz' up bookworm?" he teases, with a toothbrush hanging from his mouth. Laying my head back down, I massage my temples.

"I feel like I've been in a coma for weeks. What time is it?"

"Mornin' time."

He goes back into the bathroom and rinses out his mouth with water. He returns, wearing a new outfit. Thoroughly confused, I sit up straight, putting on my glasses.

He's wearing a dark grey long-sleeved top with thick silver trim that begins at the shoulders and neck, then comes down to the wrists and belt. Around his hip tucked neatly in a loop and tied tight, is a gold sash representing his status. His pants are black. On each hip is a holster carrying the knuckle-bracer style weapons I saw in his car's back seat. The straps are firm, causing the pants to puff out around the thighs like sweatpants, tightening at the ankles, revealing another layer of grey trim. His boots are dark with a wedge.

Ron grins.

"Cool, huh? This is my uniform."

He spins around so I get a good look at the golden Kraken symbol on his back.

"I'm the youngest Aver Bronze in the Citadel, so I kinda' like to show off."

He pulls out the bracers adjusting them around his hands.

"These bad boys are my neo-bracers."

To me, they still look like knuckle-dusters with

sharp blades on each end. I can see that they could do some serious damage to anyone on the receiving end.

"My duelling instructor, Aver Gold Poppett, gave them to me. Cool, huh?"

"Very cool."

His grin fades as he puts his bracers away. My response, it seems, isn't everything he's hoped.

"Anyway," I begin. "what age are the other trainees going to be?"

"You're in luck," he tells me. "Fledgils and Aster Bronze trainees begin as teenagers, so our equivalent of fifteen to eighteen. It can take two or more years to become an Aster Gold, another two to become Aver Bronze First Class."

He winks and walks over to my bedside, fixing up the mess of paperwork.

"Don't worry. You'll fit right in. Come on, let's get some breakfast. I don't wanna keep you holed up here for your last day of studying."

Is it the last day already? I groan internally because I'm still so ill-informed.

"Come on, let's go."

He helps me onto my feet and we make our way towards the elevators and head down to a large open area on the twenty-sixth floor where I see other students standing around, chatting and drinking a warm liquid out of white ceramic mugs with the Altair Kraken symbol on the sides.

They stare at us as we pass them, their curiosity aroused. My brother ignores them; his smile remains cheerful. Following Ron to the other side of the room, I am overawed by the number of alien species in the room. That's when it happens.

Slam! Hitting something hard, I stumble.

"Grrr. Who are you!? Tiny man!?"

The voice is like a volcano erupting in my face. I stare at a seven-foot-tall lizard man. He has a gigantic oval face with a square jaw and brown eyes with dilated pupils. His thick brown scales and huge muscles barely fit into his uniform. He has a hunchback, no tail, and huge, meaty, legs.

"Another human?" he growls, jerking in my direction.

Ron turns to the alien and smiles.

"Hey, Kiwok. What's up?"

Kiwok turns to my brother, spitting on his right boot. Ron frowns, kicking his foot, catapulting the goopy mess of spittle through the air.

"Who is this? Yes. This tiny man?" Kiwok roars.

Ron pretends to clear his ears as a joke.

"Kiwok, this is Finn, my younger brother. He's going to take the entrance exams with you."

Kiwok looks at me, filled with rage. Straightening my back, locking my legs, I'm ready to dodge a sudden attack.

"Humans only cause us trouble!" Kiwok shouts. "Father says humans..."

He pauses to find the words.

"...violent. Stupid."

Great...another Chad Brunestick.

"That's not nice, Kiwok. Don't let what your father says affect your opinion, 'kay? We're friendly!"

Kiwok stomps towards Ron, who stands firm, raising his brow.

"Dad. Hate you! Useless, stupid!"

Ron nods.

"Ya, I know."

I lean in towards Ron and reduce my voice to a whisper.

"You have enemies or something?"

He shrugs.

"Let's just say not all the other Aster Bronze ranks like me."

Kiwok is glaring at me.

"Human, you stay out of my way. You slow me down!"

With that, he lumbers through the hall, pushing others aside in the process. Suddenly feeling a hand on my shoulder, I spin on my heels, ready to defend myself, but it's Ron.

"I'm all for fighting back," he says "but we might wanna wait until you pass the entrance exams before dealing with Kiwok. Remember," he says "we came down here for the food."

He guides me across the open area to the far end where there is a vast cafeteria filled with long white tables. Floating blue disks are used as chairs with students sitting at them, studying or eating. The entire room is on a platform that ends in a sharp dip. A metal fence is in place to prevent students from falling over.

The Cafeteria's right-hand wall is transparent, giving us an incredible view of space and distant stars. The lights above us sparkle blue and white. On the far-left wall are several buffet tables, each with a selection of alien foods and an alien standing behind, serving. Ron heads for one where an alien that appears to be made of a gelatinous green ooze is serving the food.

Walking over, Ron picks up two blue plates. He hands one to me.

"Go ahead,"

The food-server looks at me and I see that she has a round, bulbous head with two white eyes floating in her face like bubbles. A smile…at least, I think it is a smile…forms from the goop as she swishes towards us.

"Ron, so nice to see you again. This must be your brother! What a charmer! What a cutie! Is he going to take the acceptance exams?"

I give a soft grin.

"Ya' he sure is."

"What's your name, love?" she asks.

My words catch in the back of my throat. Ron waits for only a second before answering her.

"His name is Finn."

"Wonderful! A great name. A unique name!"

Ron looks at me with a raised eyebrow as if to say "Go on then. Talk to her!"

"R-right." I gulp. "Thank you."

"My pleasure. Good luck with your tests! Help yourself to anything you'd like."

I give her a small grin.

"Thank you. So, what's your name?"

"I am Paypin, dear. What would you like?"

I study the foods on display to pick the ones that look the most 'Earth-like.' I point to a green square loaf, tiny pink "hash-browns" sprinkled with brown sugar, three neon-green sausage rolls with small spikes on the ends, then finally, a mug filled with "coffee".

As I point, Paypin uses a spatula-like implement to place my selections on my plate.

"Thank you." I say.

"You're welcome, Finn Bates." She answers.

At the last table, I see urns set up from which other species are filling their mugs and I fill my mug from the urn that Ron has picked. The hot, brown liquid fills me with anticipation. *Something I recognize.*

"Out of all these unfamiliar foods, I'm glad you still have coffee." I tell Ron.

He laughs as we find a seat.

"It's actually called Moon Sap. It's made from the

liquid that seeps out of plants on the tiny moons in the Palixis Galaxy."

My eyes wander to my mug. Now that he mentions it, the colour is lighter than regular coffee.

"Does it have any bad side effects?"

"Nah, man. It's literally coffee. The more Moon Sap you drink, the better. It saves the moons ecosystem by draining the excess sap."

"I'll remember that."

Bringing the mug to my lips, I take a sip and let the warm brew move down my throat, settling in my stomach. It is not quite coffee, but it is not awful either.

Looking around, I notice that, at a nearby table, a Fledgil is glaring. The resentment hidden behind that cold glare sends a shiver down my spine. I turn back to my food. My choices taste strange compared with human foods. The 'bread' is slightly sour, my "hash-browns" are sweet like chocolate but contain a hint of saltiness. I let the morsels roll about on my tongue before hesitantly swallowing them. Meanwhile, Ron scarfs his down like a garbage disposal. He goes back for seconds just as I set my knife and fork onto the plate.

I sit there, trying to take it all in. I imagine trying to describe this to my mother...

As I think of her, a chill runs down my spine and I get the distinct feeling that something isn't right at home. I try to push the thought aside, but it simply grows stronger until I feel that something is definitely wrong and that I should be there.

When Ron returns, I tell him all this, expecting him to be dismissive but he surprises me by taking me seriously.

"How sure are you?" he asks.

"Well, obviously, I can't be totally sure but the more I try to tell myself that it's my imagination, the stronger the feeling gets."

"Well, I don't know what to think," Ron says "but you've always been a smart kid. I'll be the first to trust ya'. So, what are we waiting for? Let's haul off."

He stands up and I follow him towards the exit.

"Bye, Bates brothers!" Paypin's sweet voice chimes.

In Ron's quarters, he notifies Godsonion Ulmu that he is making an "Emergency Trip to Earth" and then warns Departure Control of his E.T.D. in 15 minutes.

We grab a few things from Ron's quarters and go back to the elevators. After a moment or two, one arrives and whisks us down to Launch Bay 1A on the four hundred and forty-eighth floor where Eunoia is now docked. She looks cleaner than before.

"Great!" Ron exclaims. "Who washed my ride?"

A pink-skinned alien with yellow eyes walks past.

"It was that fire-breathing freak, Miv."

At the sound of her name, I grip the Universal Translator in my pocket.

"She's not a freak." I say.

My voice is less-than-convincing. The alien rolls her eyes, exiting through the nearest door. Ron lets out a heavy sigh, taps his Jericho Watch and lowers Euonia's entry ramp. Once inside, we settle into the cockpit. Ron activates the A.I. and has EON run through the departure checks.

"EON, engage thrusters, set course for Earth."

"Thrusters engaged. " EON's voice advises.

He triggers the communication link.

"Departure control. Windfire 901, ready for departure."

"Windfire 901," Control replies, "area decompression begins. Departure will be via bay 103 in approximately 38 seconds."

"Roger that," Ron replies.

He switches channels and addresses EON.

"EON, move to departure bay 103 and set course for Earth, Bayside Heights, Big Red Slide Park Canada B.C."

"Flight Coordinates set" EON confirms.

We manoeuvre gently towards a departure bay some way distant and hold.
The bay door opens.

"Decompression complete. Departure approved."

EON's voice announces *"Departure in 8 seconds"*.

As the countdown ends, Eunoia blasts out of the launch bay, hurtling us into space. As before, EON counts us down before we enter hyperspace. After what seems like a few moments, we exit hyperspace into the earth's mesosphere. Ron triggers the invisibility cloak.

"We don't want to be detected by the Sky-Watch Radar Network", he says as we plunge into the troposphere.

Far below us, a Boeing 747 tracks through the clouds. Moments later, Bayside Heights becomes recognizable. Our speed slows until The Big Red Slide park appears as a red blot in my vision. EON prepares us for a silent landing on the remotest edge of the park, an area which few people venture.

"Like a glove." Ron mutters.

His voice is lost to me, drowned out by the hissing of the airlock. Now safely parked, Ron peers up the hill, his brows furrowing. Following his line of sight, I spot two children getting off their bikes.

"They look a little too inquisitive for my liking.'"

They look to be nine or ten. One of the boys begins jogging down the hill.

"Ah, shouldn't we do something?" I ask.

His voice takes on an ominous tone.

"No. Trust me."

Oh god. Is the ship going to electroshock them? Are they going to get blown up?

SLAM! The first kid runs right into the front of our ship landing back-first on the grass. I wince at the sound. Looking aghast at Ron, I see that he is covering his mouth in an effort not to burst into laughter. Then the other kid follows suit- BAM! He slams into Eunoia.

The kids are stunned and bewildered but, fortunately, not seriously hurt. They stagger to their feet and go back up the hill. Both are likely going to have a few bruises. I wonder how they are going to explain it to their parents. At first, I feel bad for wanting to laugh at the thought, but I give into the temptation and chuckle. Ron is clearly thinking the same thing.

"Well, that's never happened before. Don't worry. Their parents wouldn't believe they ran into an invisible wall in a million years."

Ron opens the entrance port with the flick of a switch and the ramp slides out to the ground smoothly and silently.

"Take care, and let Mom and Dad know that I'm okay, alright?"

I'm confused.

"Aren't you coming with me? I ask.

Ron shakes his head.

"Nah! I don't think that's a good idea. Losing me once was bad enough. To lose me again, as well as you, well... you know!

"I guess." I admit. "After all, I can't tell them you are well since I'm not supposed to have seen you, let alone signed up to join you!"

"Exactly." Ron says. "but I'm sure you'll think of something!"

This is not what I expected, and the idea of facing

both Mom and Dad is frightening, especially as I have to rejoin Ron. I'm far from sure I can convince them of the truth. But Ron has a point and I recognize that I'm going to have to face this alone.

Ron pats me on the shoulder.

"You can do this little brother. Now get out of here. I've got to leave in case anyone comes to investigate the "invisible wall". I'll be back for you in 24 hours."

Reluctantly, I hoist my backpack with all my studies in them onto my shoulder and make my way slowly down the ramp.

"Good luck with the rest of studying. See ya tomorrow, round' noon?"

"Yep, sounds good. Don't sleep in, ok?"

He smiles at that, waving goodbye.

Once I am out of the ship, I see the air ripple as Euonia takes off, and although I can't see her, I shield my eyes against the swirling dust that marks her departure.

Why do I feel like this was all a dream?

Walking back home, bag on my back, I fight against the cold evening air. Glad that I wore my toque, I pull it down over my ears. My t-shirt, on the other hand, does little to protect me.

I open the basement door and am greeted by silence. Dropping my shoes onto the mat, I put my paperwork on my bed and make my way upstairs.

Puzzled, I note that all the kitchen lights are on, but I can't see anyone. Mom isn't in the living room. I go back into the kitchen. The small island had hidden Mom from view earlier, but she is leaning over the kitchen table with her head in her hands. Her long hair is hiding her expression, but she is clearly distressed, and I am filled with apprehension.

"Mom? What's wrong?"

Walking up to her, I gingerly touch her back with my hand. She turns to look up at me. She's a mess. Her cheeks are gaunt, her eyes are red, her skin pale. *I remember when her eyes used to be so bright...*

"Mom, what happened?"

Tears remain in the corners of her eyes. At the sound of my voice, they roll down her cheeks. She sobs. I put my arms around her and pull her close to my chest. It's always been like this. Mom hides her desperation for months, letting it fester until it eventually boils over. Dad has never been here for her, so I've had to take his place.

"I'm sorry, Finn."

"It's ok, mom."

It doesn't matter what the problem is, I'll hold her until she feels better.

Mom cries for another minute or two before pulling away and wiping her face. Grabbing a paper towel from a roll on the counter, she brings it to her nose, blowing into it.

"I just...I just need to apologize to you."

"You haven't done anything wrong, mom. I'm ok."

I try to give her my best smile, but her frown shows she doesn't buy it.

"Ever since Ron disappeared that night, we all know I haven't been the same. I don't give you as much attention and care as I should, but it's not your fault it's mine."

I don't want to hear this, especially now that I know that Ron is alive.

"Mom..." I whisper. "I understand. Please, don't be so upset." I beg.

Seeing mom like this breaks my heart. She makes her way to the trash-can under the sink, throwing away her soiled towelette.

"Your father called. I don't know how to tell you this, but...he doesn't want to come home."

"Come, home? What does he mean by that?"

"He wants us to divorce. He says that he doesn't want to be a part of this family anymore. "

"Divorce?" I gasp.

"Yes. I know. It's a terrible blow but we couldn't go on the way we were so it's probably for the best really."

Clenching my fists together, I bite my lower lip. It takes every bit of self-control not to throw a temper tantrum.

"How could he do this?" I demand angrily. "I mean, I'm not deaf or blind. I know that things have not been going well between you lately but it's not your fault that Ron went missing. The only reason Dad wants to drown himself in work is that he misses Ron! And now he wants a divorce because he thinks things won't get better."

I'm furious, not only over Dad's selfish attitude but because of the horrendous situation I am now in. I am completely torn.

Not only is Ron alive and I can bring him back, if he comes, but we are both sworn to Altair and, in less than twenty four hours, I will also be gone. Mom will be on her own.

Mom reaches out, fixing my glasses, which are slowly falling off my face. Underneath them, she can see my tears pooling.

"Finn.", she whispers, "I promise this isn't your fault. As people age, feelings change, for better or for worse. Your father feels that he needs to do something with his life...it just..." she chokes. "...it doesn't include us."

"Mom," I start, "Did this problem begin when Ron disappeared or were there problems before?"

Mom looks at me, surprised.

"Well, things weren't perfect. I mean, I would have liked him to be home more often, but I knew he travelled when I married him. But you are right. When Ron disappeared, and all the searches failed to find him, your father went into a deep depression and we seemed to spend most of our time, when he was home, arguing and fighting. I hated it but nothing I said or did seemed to please him."

I take a deep breath and think hard about what I need to say next.

"Mom, please understand that this is a very long shot, but what if I could find Ron and bring him home?"

Mom gasps.

"What are you talking about? How could you bring him home?"

"I can't explain, you'll just have to trust me, but I think that I might have a way of finding him. If I can, I'll try to bring him home."

"If you have a way to do that, why haven't you done it before? You know how worried I've been."

"Because I have only just worked out how it can be done, but only if I am lucky...and there is a downside. I will be gone for a while. I'm not sure how long but, if this works out, you'll have us both back to look after you."

Mom takes a second to gather herself.

"Finn, this is hard to believe, but...you've always been the smartest one in the family."

She smiles.

"Alright, I'll take you at your word. But promise me that you, at least, will come back. I couldn't bear losing both of you."

"You won't, but I'll have to start tomorrow."

Mom looks shocked.

"So soon? Couldn't you stay a little longer?"

"You know I'd like to, Mom, but if this is to work, I have to get started right away."

I take her in my arms and give her a huge hug.

"Mom, I promise you that I'll do my very best. Now you go to bed and try to get some sleep. I have some work to do."

"Very well, son, I'll try. Don't stay up too late, will you?"

"I'll be fine, Mom. Goodnight"

"Goodnight...and thank you."

Mom heads off to her bedroom and I go down into my own room, flopping face-down on the bed, shoving my head into my pillow in pure frustration.

I know, deep down, this shouldn't be a surprise. Things have been tense between my parents for a long time, like a rope being pulled in opposite directions from each end. Today. That rope finally snapped. *But to have Dad say he doesn't want anything to do with us?* Even if he does change his mind, the damage has been done. *I'm not one to quickly forget when people hurt me or my family.*

However, right now, I need to find a way to distract myself from this troubling situation. Sitting on the edge of my bed, I mentally collect myself, washing my face in the downstairs washroom. Getting changed into some comfortable clothes, I sit cross legged on the floor. Flipping open the training manual, I read the lines of text with new-found determination. *If I can't bring Ron back for both my parents, I'll have to do it for mom. That way, I'll finally see her smile again...*

When 3 am comes, I'm lying in the fetal position on my mattress. I'm still not prepared for my exams. *Duh.* Here are the issues I've run into, boiled down to two points.

First, the exam will be written in an alien language called Citadelus, formed by the High Council to seamlessly communicate between races. *Guess what?* I can't read Citadelus,

Second, I only managed to get through a little over three-quarters of the book.

I feel a sudden, overwhelming sense of dread. I close the book, setting it aside. I attempt to let the calm of the silent nighttime air ease my tension. *It's no use! Not only will I be under-educated tomorrow, but I will also be lacking sleep.*

I shuffle under my blankets and am about to close my eyes when I notice that something has fallen out of my pants pocket when I tossed them on the floor. I pad across the carpeted floor and crouch on my knees. With a grin, I see that it is the move memorizer chip.

"I forgot to keep this on Altair." *I hope I don't get in trouble for this.* I roll the tiny chip between my fingertips, resting it on my palm. *Miv gave this to me to help with the physical exam, but I can't even wear it for more than a second.* I bite my lower lip chewing furiously at the loose skin. I turn back to the book. *Will it help me memorize this text and can I bear the pain long enough for it to work?* Only one way to find out.

I guess tomorrow will give me the answer...

A ROBOT BEATS ME UP IN A BOXING MATCH

My head is face-down in my pillow. Sitting up on my elbows, I groan. A vast red mark has formed on my right cheek. Massaging the tenseness out of my jaw, waiting for the redness to go away, I roll onto my back, slide to the edge of the mattress, and stand up to shake away the cobwebs. My back is sore. I stretch, rotating my joints until they feel well-oiled and ready to work. I glance at my bedside clock. It's eleven-forty.

Oh...no! I have about twenty minutes to meet Ron at the park. Throwing on my jeans and long sleeve shirt, I grab the book and my notes, stuffing them into my pack and racing for the front door where my shoes are still on the mat. Levering them on, I look around the house. It's silent other than for my laboured breathing. *Wish me, luck mom...*

Then I'm out of the door and charging down the hill. My shoes slap onto the concrete, *Please Ron, you better not leave without me!*

Ten minutes pass, I'm still two blocks away from the park and my lungs are about to burst. My glasses have misted up so the figures ahead of me are just blurs.

Stumbling into the park, I rush down the grassy hill, tripping once or twice on the frosted ground, causing cold water to soak into the back of my pants.

Here, right? My feet slide. Bang! They collide with Eunoia's exterior. From within the ship, I swear I can hear Ron laughing.

With a quiet hiss, the entrance hatch slides open and the ramp deploys. I stagger aboard and see that Ron has a broad grin on his face.

"What did you think I was gunna do?" he says. "Abandon you if ya' slept in a little?"

"W- well, I don't know! Besides, it's not my fault. My feet slipped."

"Uh-huh." Nodding, he waves me in.

We move up to the cockpit and I collapse into the passenger seat while Ron engages EON ready for launch.

"Don't get too comfy in that seat." Ron warns me. "We gotta' get you changed into your Fledgil's uniform, ready for the exam."

He winks.

"You ready to show 'em who's boss?"

I open my mouth to respond, but he rambles on.

"Speaking of that, how'd your studyin' go?"

I feign confidence, giving a tight grin with wide eyes.

"Oh, it went...awesome."

Ron gives me a knowing look.

"I'll believe ya'. EON, are we clear to launch?"

"Clear. Hatches sealed. Internal pressure in the green. Ready for launch in ten."

"Do it," Ron says.

There is barely any sensation as we lift off and are soon passing through the stratosphere. Ron turns to look at me.

"Let's go down to the crew deck. While you are changing, tell me about mom?"

We go down and he doesn't seem to notice my hesitation as Eunoia enters the darkness of space. *The news of a divorce will break his heart. I can't tell him the truth yet!*

She just..." *cried herself to sleep-* "-wanted to talk about school, like I guessed."

"Cool beans." Relief washes over me. *I've avoided the drama, for now.*

I get changed into my shirt. The material is comfy. *But man, they could have picked a smaller size? I'm swimming in this thing!*

EON announces our transition to hyperdrive, and it doesn't seem so long this time before we decelerate for our arrival at Altair and go through the landing formalities. As we settle in the landing bay, I'm reminded that the time has come for me to take my exams. This is a huge deal, and I am extremely nervous.

We go up to his room so I can drop my pack.

"Exams are in an hour, got any questions?" Ron asks.

"Ya"

I fish through my jean pocket.

"Is it ok if I wear this during the tests?"

I show him the Move Memorizer. His hand forms a thumbs up.

"Just keep it discrete, know what I mean, jellybean?"

His lingo irritates me.

"Er- no, I don't. Can I use this or not?"

"Technically no." he tells me, "-but you're a rare case. Without battle training, you're at a disadvantage. Using unregulated Altair tech will level the playing field."

Following behind Ron, we join the swarming students morphing in-and-out of the elevators. The volume of their chatter sets my teeth on edge, as I try to keep up with my brother.

Ron rubs his hands together with eagerness.

"Alright, the exam room is on floor 444. I'll take you to the registration desk, but after that, you're on your own."

I move around some aliens, each about the size of my head, as they scurry between my feet looking rather alarmed.

"Where will you be?"

"Watching. Aver Bronze ranks oversee the exams."

Well, that's a slight comfort. If Ron is scoring my test, maybe he'll cheat and give me an A+.

We cram into an elevator, stepping out at floor 444. We're greeted by a snaking-line of trainees waiting to get into a huge room. A set of large metal doors are propped open and, at a white table, two tree-like humanoids are taking student information. Ron looks down at me. I must look absolutely terrified because his eyes soften, and he pats me on the back.

"You can do this, Finn. It's not just me cheering for you. Remember that. Now get your butt in that lineup!"

He heads down to the other end of the hall, exiting via a sliding door and disappearing from my sight. *Who else is rooting for me? I thought everybody hated humans.* The comment leaves me puzzled.

Getting into the lineup, I keep my eyes glued to the floor, knitting my hands together like a polite schoolgirl. Somebody shoves into me. Turning around I glare. It's another large student with two heads and black eyes.

"Hiss!"

"Sorry!"

I turn away. *I wonder if having two brains is cheating?*

At last, I reach the front of the line. Another Aver Gold is sitting in front of a screen, checking in each student. This one has a body that appears to be assembled from oak-wood, and long slender arms tipped with beautiful pinkish-blue leaves.

It is clearly female. She has a long thin mouth and grey eyes.

"Oh my, a human?"

Her voice is soft and non-judgmental.

"Yes, ma'am,"

"Well, Godsonion Ulmu is a trusted recruiter. He wouldn't have brought you here if he didn't think you had the right stuff."

She smiles, pointing down at a pale square scanner set into the table.

"Just scan your fingerprint." she says, taking my forefinger. I put it on the scanner. It buzzes, then pings!

Pulling away, her screen switches to a school picture of my face alongside a large file of personal information. *Good thing I've never done anything illegal.*

"How do you guys have all this?"

She tilts her head.

"Once we have your D.N.A. in the system, we can find any information on you in the known galaxies. This helps the Citadel keep track of all recruits."

She swipes the screen, and a black line appears.

"Go ahead and sign, Finn Bates from planet Earth."

I hesitate for a second before using a stylus to sign my name on the touchscreen.

"Thank you."

She glances at a silver chip with a number stamped into it.

"Desk fifty, row five. Good luck." She says as she hands me the chip.

Entering the room, I am stunned by the number of students sitting at the rows and rows of blue desks. The tabletops are computer screens. At this moment, each screen displays a desk number. I find row five, number fifty and settle down in the uncomfortable plastic chair. The room is cold and the atmosphere tense. Many Fledgils' share concerned expressions, *just like good old high-school days.*

Somebody sits in the chair next to me. She appears to be a half-cat person. Taking the silver chip given to her, she slides it into a slot on the desk and the computer screen changes to a notice that *"The exam will begin in ten minutes."* Beneath it, there is a countdown clock that is unnerving.

Doing the same, my chip fires up the computer.

Now, all I have to do is wait. The room fills up. On the front wall, a large digital clock is glowing like a beacon.

Ulmu appears from a side door and takes the chair at the centre of a table at the front of the room, facing the students. Four more Aver Bronze staff enter. These include my brother. He scans the room until he spots me. I raise an eyebrow while shrugging. He responds with a nod and then takes his designated spot beside Ulmu.

Next to Ron, a lizard-like-alien, possibly eight feet tall thwumps onto his seat. The chair cracks beneath him. He growls, then scans the room until he spots me. His eyes lock onto me, glaring.

He looks exactly like Kiwok! That must be Woya, the aforementioned father that hates Ron.

Ulmu stands up, and the room falls silent.

"I am delighted that so many of you have applied to join our ranks. Though many of you won't pass, we still appreciate your drive and your wish to protect our known galaxies to the best of your abilities. Good luck."

His elongated finger points up at the clock.

"You have an hour to finish this exam."

He drops his hand as the count-down clock on the wall reaches zero.

"Begin!"

I'm like a rat trapped in a cage. I stare at my screen as it lights up with a series of yes-or-no formatted questions.

Wait...this is in English! I thought everything was written in Citadelus? A smile forms on my face. *Ulmu's saved my butt again.*

The first question reads, *"The planet Dree is primarily water. Do the residents of this planet live above ground? Yes or No"*

With every single question, I'm forced to use my tablet's note-taking tab, scribbling down my thoughts. After thirty questions, the world turns into a silent blur. At the twenty-minute mark, I hear a number of students get up and leave the gymnasium, the squeaking of their chairs a slight distraction.

I'm on a section where I have to chart out planet locations on a Citadel map.

So...if Othinda protects A-G. No, was that Vusta? Groaning, I bite my lip, picking at the skin. Choosing an answer, I move to the next question. Some minutes later, the entire row on my left has completed their exam. One alien two seats away, quits in rage, storming out of the gym. I finish three more questions, arriving at the final section.

Suddenly, the room is hushed. I haven't looked up from my tablet for some time. My head is heavy, yet I manage to gawk up at the clock...*only ten minutes left!* I blink, Ron and Ulmu are looking at me. *I'm the only one left!*

The anxiety of being the center of attention crawls across my skin like insects. Shivering, I make eye contact with my elder brother.

Remember why you're here, Finn.

Looking back at the final section of my test, I shut out the world. The clock ticks down. I complete another answer.

Only a few more minutes left!

The sentences are swimming across my vision like swarms of fish.

Last question!

"That will be all, Finn."

Great, I didn't finish...

Putting down my stylus, I stare at the computer, riddled with frustration. It goes to a white screen with black font. *"Thank you for your participation!"* I figure that, for sure, I have failed.

Taking a deep breath, I rise from my seat. Ulmu's hands knit together, his head resting upon them. Ron has a proud look on his face but it doesn't reassure me. Stepping out into the hallway, I see other students staring at me as they chuckle under their breath. At this point, I'm choking on my self-pity.

"What a waste of time…"

That's when I hear a voice from within the gym.

"What?!"

Curiosity gets the better of me; I peek into the gym.

Kiwok's father is standing over my desk, staring at my notes.

"This is insane!? What is this human nonsense?"

Ron crosses the gymnasium, a terrifying glare on his usually cheerful face.

"Why don't ya' back off a bit, Woya? It's not your job to score the tests!"

Ulmu stands up, crossing his arms.

"Enough, both of you!"

Woya turns on his heels, snorting at Ron while talking to Ulmu.

"We can't allow this, can we? Ron's brother is clearly brainless!"

Ulmu's response is precise as a sniper.

"Aver Woya, I will not discriminate against a trainee because of your personal disposition."

The Godsonion stalks forward, brushing Ron aside, glaring up at Woya as his voice takes on a hint of danger.

"What you are looking at on that tablet is a boy determined to pass. Bates was given a mere two days to study our materials. One would call such knowledgeable-improvisation miraculous."

He gestures at my computer.

Woya opens his huge lizard mouth to protest- but his black eyes find me eavesdropping.

Time to go! Jumping back into the hallway, I slam into a female trainee. She's the same height as me, staring with large green eyes and grey pupils. She appears to be human, with soft pink skin and peach lips. She smiles.

"Sounds like the Godsonion likes you." Her voice is sweet as honey. With that, she walks off.

ΔΔΔ

Moments pass. I realize that Ron will not be returning to escort me to the next exam location. I'll have to strike out on my own. Merging into the crowd, I follow, carried along in the current.

An announcement plays over the loudspeakers. The voice is eerily familiar; *perhaps it's the man who greeted us into H.Q.? Phender Clubb?*

"The Physical exam will be taken on this floor, Room 62, Gymnasium 2B."

He repeats the announcement twice. Making my way along the corridor, I'm squashed by a number of trainees laughing and jesting; they seem confident in their ability to pass the tests. I stare at their claws, sharp teeth, armoured bodies and keen eyes.

Suddenly, I find a large group of other Fledgils blocking my path. Beyond their shoulders and heads, I can see that the training bay door remains closed. A Phender, with a black sash across his uniform, allows one student into the gym at a time. The sound-proof doors shut, cutting us off from any clue as to what is happening inside.

Swallowing my fears, I stand at the tail end of the group as we creep forward. A long time passes. The students around me are growing increasingly anxious; nobody comes out of the gym once they enter. *Where do they go?*

When my turn finally arrives, I stare at the Phender guarding the entrance.

He has blue leathery skin with large black spots around his neck and arms, A set of five tiny tentacles layer the back of his head, paired with a thin fish mouth and a set of gills. His shirt is black, with a series of silver buttons. His hands have four webbed fingers and his belly-fat protrudes over his belt. When he sees me, he raises his hands in the air in surprise.

"Ah! You must be Finn Bates. A pleasure to meet ya' my boy!"

"Hello...sir'"

The stranger reaches out, shaking my hand. He leaves a slime coat on my palm. I wipe the cold fluid on my pants.

"Listen, boy' ya' gunna do great."

He pumps his fist against his burly chest.

"My name is Phender Whelcome. If ya' pass your exams, imma' be yer' Weapons Instructor. Along with my best friend, Socrates!"

More names for me to remember. He prattles on as I shake my head. *He's just like Ron...*

"I teach all tha' newbies."

Whelcome clears his throat.

"When Ron told me' ya' were on yer' way, I brushed up on my' human slang right away. That way yer' not gunna' have to worry bout' fallin' behind in ma' class, home dog! Haha!"

Whelcome laughs like Santa Clause, giving me a hearty pat on the back.

"Now get in er' rockstar!"

The door opens. His wet hands shove me on the shoulder.

"Wait, what's going to happen once I'm inside?!"

But by the time I turn around to protest, the door is already closing in my face; the tip of my nose inches away from being flattened like a pancake.

I spin around. Before me is a ginormous gymnasium dominated by a twenty-foot window. The floor is lined with blue shock-absorbing mats stamped with Altair's signature Kraken. They are sprinkled with broken mechanical pieces and blood. A shiver ripples through me, as I turn to face a familiar group of faces at the desk. Sitting in order are Woya, two unknown soldiers, Godsonion Ulmu and Ron. Woya snorts while shaking his head.

"Step onto the mats boy, let's get this over with!"

"Hush Woya!" Ulmu snaps.

The Godsonion turns back to me.

"Now Finn," he begins. "the physical exam is simple. You will face one of our training bots on the lowest setting. Simply defend yourself to the best of your abilities. We will judge."

Ron leans forward.

"Just kick it in the robo-junk"

Ulmu closes his eyes at this crude comment.

Woya hisses "Shut it, Bates!"

"Come at me, lizard-breath!" Ron counters.

Their bickering is cut short by Ulmu's blood-freezing glare. Ron sits back in his chair, crossing his arms.

"S- sorry, sir."

Ulmu sighs, pointing across the room. Lining the wall are tall silver robots, with flat faces and limbs covered in white fabric padding. Raising his wrist, he taps his Jericho Watch and a training-bot whirrs to life. It lumbers into the center of the room several feet away, raising its arms and pivoting its feet.

My hands find the Move Memorizor and I activate the chip.

"This model uses a four-step attack sequence." Ulmu hints. "Good luck."

The robot springs to life, raising its left fist and moving lightly over the blue mats. I am taking a deep breath inwards when the robot's fist cracks against my jaw. An intense stinging sensation sends me flying backwards. I land on my side, the padding doing little to brace my fall.

"Augh-"

My cold hand lingers upon my swollen jaw. Woya snorts again. I look up at him. His arms are crossed in confidence. Ulmu remains silent, his eyes calm and watchful. Ron gives me his trademark thumbs-up, *Nice, bro, real helpful.*

"Beep boop?"

The robot hesitates as if confused by my lack of practice. I rise to my feet as the training-bot attacks again with the same right-sided punch. It careens sideways, slamming me on the other side of my face. With a sickening crack! I hit the floor, eyes shut with humiliation and pain. I can feel my face swelling.

Don't give up now, only two more moves to go, then I'll know the entire combo!

"This is agonizing-" a random Avter Gold with rainbow skin comments.

"Clearly the boy has no battle experience."

A flood of determination courses through me.

"No!" I shout, stamping my feet onto the mat, staggering to face my opponent.

"I'm not done yet!"

Not waiting to see their reactions, I face my enemy as the robot starts with his right hook. I dodge. *Here comes the left hook.* I duck but the robot's right leg lifts making direct contact with my core. Sputtering out spit and air, I fall over, pain coursing through me.

Ulmu seems deep in thought.

"That will be enough Fi…"

My hand shoots into the air, my thumb stuck high in the sky.

"I'm ok!"

Behind the spots dancing in my vision, the Altair higher-ups watch as I rise again. Fresh blood coats my lip from a small incision. Staring at Ulmu, a wave of calm washes over me.

"Trust me."

The robot jumps on the mat, beginning his rotation full throttle. Firing up every muscle in my body, I dodge both punches, barrel-rolling from the leg kick. It's other leg rises, nailing me in the ribs, sending white-hot pain through my core, but I hold my ground, grabbing the robot's leg, pushing it away. I trigger the A.I to begin the sequence once more. *Now's my chance!*

Straining at the training bot with all my waning strength, the moment feels akin to David sizing up Goliath. I tap my Move Memorizer and a burst of electricity flows to my brain. I feel galvanized and see a ripple of confusion cross the judge's faces. Only Ron's expression is that of pride.

The robot charges. With the enemy sequence memorized, I easily slip-slide from its attacks. The surge of electricity leaves every cell in my body shaking with anticipation.

"Take this!"

As with Miv's demonstration, my body moves on its own, raising my left first, the knuckles' slam across the sharp curve of the robot's jaw. It bleeps and bloops. My fingers crack under the pressure but I ignore the pain. *I'll pass this test. No matter what!*

Slamming it with my fist tightly clenched, I deal the same damage it was programmed to do to me. Its gears grind beneath my bare-knuckles and it falls off the mat, crashing onto the metal floor; gears spit out of its back. As it starts to get back up to its feet, I knee it in the gut, and it falls to one knee.

I've never won a battle before and it feels amazing! Damaged wires and crushed mechanical joints tumble from beneath my sneaker.

"How's this for an attack, Tin-can?"

Spinning into a roundhouse, I land the death

blow. My foot breaks the robot's ribcage and sparks explode from its insides. It falls over with a satisfying crash! My legs go limp and I slip onto my knees, my fingers digging into the soft fabric.

Is it...over?

I JOIN THE LOSERS CLUB

"Finn, are you ok!?"

Ron vaults over the table, rushing to my side. His hands find my shoulders pulling me into an upright sitting position. His large brown eyes scan my wounds with a frown.

"Darn, you really took one for the team, huh?"

A slamming sound startles me. My shoulders tense with anticipation. Woya's fists are planted on the table, its legs trembling from the weight.

"Impossible!" Woya roars, rounding the table while his forked tongue flicks in irritation.

"You have no battle experience, Finn Bates, you cheated!"

Ron rises to the challenge.

"Maybe you shouldn't underestimate him, you

fat lug!"

Woya flashes his fangs while flexing his legs.

My hand grips Ron's wrist.

"Stop! It's ok. He can think what he wants."

Crossing the floor, Ulmu finds my broken glasses.

"Very mature of you, Finn. Not the result that our friend Woya expected, clearly."

Woya fumes but cannot go against Ulmu. He utters a furious grunt and storms back to the judges table, slumping in his seat.

Ron holds out his hand, helping me to my feet.

"Come on. There is an infirmary above us where we can treat your injuries."

"I will go with you." Ulmu says, surprising both Ron and me.

Watching Woya as I walk, my gaze is unflinching. *I'll bide my time as Ron suggested earlier.*

As we approach the elevators, I see that one is waiting for us with its doors open. I assume that, as Godsoion, Ulmu can summon the nearest elevator at any time. He strides into the open car and we follow.

"Hey," Ron whispers in my right ear, "that was so cool!"

"Well, thanks, but it didn't feel that cool. My face is going to hurt for weeks."

The tender skin is hot to the touch and terribly inflamed.

Four floors up, Ulmu leads us into Main Infirmary which treats minor wounds for all species. The other three medical floors are for the specialized needs of specific species. With Ulmu leading us, we are able to bypass "triage" and proceed directly to a long, white-walled room lined with hovering beds all neatly made up and surrounded by unfamiliar equipment. A tiny robot comes gliding from underneath a medicine cabinet that is fitted with an arrangement of colorful bottles. It has metal ball-like "head" than can swivel and twin lenses.

Ulmu sees my look of amazement.

"This little machine uses those lenses to create a three-dimensional image for transmission to a diagnostic array which then instructs it how to proceed."

Lo-and-behold, the little robot also speaks to me. It's large robot "eyes" gaze up at me.

"Hello! I am a medico 7D. I will treat your injuries!"

It parks beside one of the beds.

"Sit please."

I can't help smiling at the little guy who reminds me of a cute animal, but I do as it says

Ulmu smiles.

"These medical bots ensure that staff remain healthy and in peak condition."

"Well, if it can stop my jaws aching, that'd be great."

"You'll be just fine. You'll see."

Ron bites his lower lip, a universal Bates-family gesture. The bot rolls in front of me. It presses a button on the bed, and I'm lowered to match its diminutive height. Two arms appear from slots on the sides of its body, and then the chest opens, revealing a tiny silver spray canister.

"Please close your eyes and hold your breath!" it instructs me.

I do so and I'm sprayed in the face with an odourless liquid that congeals as it touches my skin..Curious, I lick my lips, tasting something medicinal.

"MA-G is a gel-spray, infused with micro-bot technology. It is absorbed through the skin and deployed to heal wounds and soothe pain, such as throbbing, headaches, swelling." Ulmu explains.

I become aware of the numbing sensation that the MA-G is having on me. The wounds from my punches are reduced to a light throb; the cut on my lip closes completely.

"So, MA-G is an abbreviation for?"

This time, it is the micro-bot that answers my question.

"Micro-Adhesive healing Gel. All significant wounds have been healed. Thank you for your time!"

With that, it glides off back to its station under the cabinet, collapsing into a tiny metal box. My eyes find Godsonion Ulmu's. His expression is unreadable.

Thinking back to my thrashing, I'm feeling despondent.

"I understand my performance was unremarkable, but if I was like the other students, I could have ripped my opponent apart with my teeth or claws. But we humans aren't built like that. Still, I hope you will still consider recruiting me as an Aster. I can get stronger!"

Meeting his eyes, I'm astonished to find him smiling.

"Finn, just like every species, each Altair student

has their own individual strengths and weaknesses. Just now, you managed to show us all where your true strengths lie."

I stare at him. *Is this good or bad?*

"Do not fret, Finn. Your performance was remarkable. That being said, be aware that, at the moment, your own insecurities are a greater weakness than the fact that you are lacking teeth or claws."

Ulmu raises his hand, cupping my ear and finds the Move Memorizor which he detaches from my skin. My heart hammers in my throat, but he simply grins down at the object.

"Miv!" he chuckles. "She's always looking out for the underdogs."

His eyes flick between Ron and me.

"I will leave you two now. There are still exams to conduct."

He strides out of the room and the door closes behind him.

"Well, lookie! You got a fan."

I'm more concerned about losing my glasses. Ron's facial features are a slight blur behind a veil of lights.

"Never mind. We can soon fix that. Now, why

don't we get a treat? For showing us all who's boss!"

△△△

The treat is ice-cream. The cafeteria is crowded by trainee's chatting about the exams. Ron and I attempt to find a seat, which is no easy task. Pushing our way through the crowd, we eventually find a spot in the center of the room.

Ron braves the crowd, reappearing with two blue bowls. He slides one across the table like a bartender. This is the first food item I've seen which completely resembles something from the earth. The red, white, and brown swirls invite me to dig in. Grabbing my spoon, I scoop it into my mouth. Ron is already chowing down on his own bowl as he stares at me, trying to contain his excitement.

Expecting Neapolitan flavour, my jaw drops.

"Ah! It's sour."

Ron licks his spoon. "You'll get used to it."

Just as I finish my last bite, a buzzing sound can be heard over the crowd.

"Do you hear that? What is it?" I ask.

Before Ron can answer, a tiny drone flies over the railing scanning the crowd with a blueish-grey beam. The students smile, nudging one another expectantly.

"That's a messenger bot."

Ron's spoon clatters into his empty bowl.

"Somebody here passed their exam."

The drone continues to cruise slowly over the cafeteria tables. It appears to be moving towards the centre of the room where Ron and I are sitting.

It couldn't possibly be looking for me...could it?!

Apparently it could. It homes in on me and projects a beam that catches my eyes, causing me to blink. The drone skips over waiting students like a flat rock on water and comes to a halt before me as the room goes silent. I stare at Ron, wondering what to do. My throat turns dry as hundreds of frustrated eyes are staring at us.

"Press that red button on the front with your finger."

I do as he says, and a robotic voice announces:

"This is a message for Finn Bates. Congratulations! You have passed the entrance exam. A package will be waiting in your assigned quarters. Please confirm you have received this message."

"Uh, yes! M ...message received" I stutter.

I turn to look at Ron in amazement.

"I...did it?"

Ron smiles, nodding vigorously.

"Duh! Why wouldn't you?"

"Because he human!"

I know this booming voice. Turning around, Kiwok towers over me.

"I should have gotten a message first! You just think you special? Grrr"

He grinds his monstrous jaw together, puffing out his chest. A flash of anger crosses Ron's face, launching him from his seat. His hands slam against the table rattling our empty bowls.

"Enough Kiwok, Finn is an Aster now. Besides, I'm sure you'll get the good news soon enough. Don't go picking fights. That's an order."

Kiwok snarls.

"No! **You** be nice," he snaps. "My father is first-class too. You don't want to get on my bad side."

I can see that Ron is about to say something that he will likely regret. My stomach twists but I jump in. I actually spin to face Kiwok. My fists clench.

"I'm not here to make enemies...and you don't get to talk to us like this!"

"Really?" He growls. "You just here because Ulmu have a soft spot for humans!"

As if!

"I know why I'm here, and it's not because somebody else is forcing me. Don't assume to know my agenda!"

God, this really is Chad all over again! I'm used to being belittled but not like this in front of all the other students. It just makes me furious! I'm self-observant enough to know that the adrenaline from the previous tests has me on edge.

"Stupid human. All bark, no bite!"

Kiwok raises his arms, his fleshy palms facing my chest.

"What?" I say threateningly. "You want to fight me?"

Instinct screams that this is a super-duper-ultra bad idea, *but I don't care.*

"Let's do this!" Kiwok roars aiming to shove me. Every muscle in his body seems tense. I raise my arms to guard myself, but Ron intervenes.

"Enough!"

Grabbing Kiwok's left wrist in a vice grip, Ron's hand wraps halfway around Kiwok's thick leather skin.

"That's an order. Back down, or I'll report ya' to Ulmu. Capeesh?"

The scales around Kiwok's eyes squish as he flashes his teeth.

"Chitter!"

A four-legged figure the size of my leg catapults from the floor, landing on Kiwok's shoulder. The lizard-man freezes, turning to gawk at the cat-like creature with long white fur and bright blue eyes. The stranger's mouth opens, revealing a tiny pink tongue below sharp teeth, their paws knead Kiwok's shoulder pad.

"Why don't you back off, Kiwok?"

Her voice is chipmunk-ish. She stands up on her hind legs, using her left arm to lean against Kiwok's tiny ears. She's wearing an Aster's uniform with a white sash, and little black boots around her paws. Kiwok's face scrunches.

"Grrr! Nuyen, get off!"

He swats at the creature but Nuyen backflips off his shoulder, landing on the nearest table with all the grace of an acrobat. She rises, standing just three feet tall. Her long white tail swishes playfully.

"Why don't you pick on somebody your own size for once, you big bully!"

Kiwok is a bulldozer, looking to flatten anything in his path.

"I'll squash you flat, little Purrinan!"

Why does this guy want to pick a fight with everybody in the room!?

Just as I think things can't get crazier, two more students circle a nearby table to stand on either side of Nuyen. Various other Altair students form a semi-circle around them. Glancing at Ron, I see that he seems just as confused by the situation as I am.

One of Nuyen's new companions speaks up.

"It's okay, Kiwok! We get it. You like showing off. Big deal."

The man is wearing an Aver uniform with a gold sash. He has two shoulder-length head-tails and light blue skin. His eyes shine a brilliant yellow. His lips are dark purple, and a square tribal mark is tattooed on his chin. His ears are pointed like those of an elf.

"Nuyen's gonna claw your eyes out, and you know it."

Glancing over at the second newcomer, I'm startled to realize that she's the one I bumped into after the written exam. She has head-tails similar to her companion. They're coloured, with beautiful indigo gradients from the tips to the crown. She's also wearing an Fledgils shirt. She places her hand on her hip in a sassy pose.

"You heard my brother! Go away Kiwok."

Kiwok glares at the three of them.

"Losers. You no scare me."

He looks back towards me.

"Not over...tiny human."

Pivoting on his heels, he storms through the crowd, lumbering like a Titan down the hallway, before disappearing behind a set of doors.

Un-clenching my jaw, I loosen my shoulders.

"That was close!"

Unbeknownst to me, I have been holding my breath for the last three minutes. I let the rush of nervous air out of my lungs, glancing at the trio as the other students behind them return to their meals.

"Thank you."

The strangers nod. I turn to the humanoid alien that I ran int before.

"My name is Finn Bates, I'm the idiot who crashed into you earlier"

She chuckles. "Well, it was one way of introducing yourself. I'm Naki, by the way."

"Pleased to meet you, Naki"

Nuyen spots a group leaving a table nearby and leaps onto it.

"Chitter! Hey dudes, let's take a seat!"

We all hurry and gather round the vacated space. Naki smiles.

"I'm glad to see you're an Aster now, Finn, hopefully I'm next."

Nuyen's tail flicks.

"Chitter, I'm already an Aster. Trust me, it doesn't get easier! Gotta' fight off bullies like Kiwok a lot. Chit-chit."

Turning to look at her, I smile.

"Thank you for backing us up, by the way; you were really brave."

Her ears perk.

"Me? Hah! You're the one who challenged Kiwok to a fight in the first place!" she chimes. "Besides, it's all good. No worries, chitter!"

She winks, small tufts of loose fur falling onto the tabletop.

"Kiwok likes to pick on us small fry because his dad, Woya, is some higher up, chitchit."

Nuyen's tail wraps around her boots as she plops into a sitting position.

"I know-" I tell her. "-I've met him and he doesn't any humans." The memory of Woya's glare sends a shiver down my spine.

"But you guys don't look like small fry to me?" I add.

Kisoi laughs. "Thanks, but...trust me, we are."

"Why help us out, though?" Ron tells them. "I mean, I do appreciate it n' all."

Naki looks at him. Her huge green eyes sparkle.

"Well, Ron, we figured you guys needed some friends. Sitting alone all the time is bound to get boring, right?"

We smile at the trio.

"Yep!" Naki says. "Welcome to the losers' club! Now you have some friends."

Friends...I like the sound of that.

Naki's pointed ear twitches and her head swivels. We follow suit and hear what Naki's keen ears have picked up. Making its way in our direction is another messenger bot. The beam hits Naki head-on, beelining towards her. Without hesitation, Naki taps the interface.

"This is a message for Naki Belle. Congratulations, you have passed the entrance exam. A package will be waiting for you in your assigned quarters. Please confirm you have received this message."

Naki positively chitters with surprise and delight.

"Message received", she manages.

Kisoi pats his little sister on the back, glowing with pride.

"I've been training Naki for many years, so this is a big moment for her"

The glow in Kisoi's bright yellow eyes shows he never doubted Naki for a second.

Nuyen makes a guttural sound in her throat.

"Congrats Naki! I became an Aster one month ago. Can't wait for classes to start."

Naki smiles with her lips shut. Indigo blush forms on her light pink cheeks; her radiance glows from across the table.

"Thank you Nuyen." She grabs her head-tails, positioning them in front of her shoulder pads. She turns her attention to Ron.

"So, Ron, I've seen you around before. My brother always talks about you."

Kisoi smiles. "In a good way."

"Yes," she confirms. "You're trying to make the earth a Known Planet, correct?"

Ron nods. "And I need help. That's why Finn is here." He glances at me, then back at our new friends. "It's been a few years; I'll admit I ain't any closer to my goal."

Nuyen curls up on the table.

"Well, Ron, we support you!"

Kisoi and Naki nod in agreement, causing Ron's eyes to light up. *This must be the first time that people have shown support for him.*

Five more messenger bots come flying into the cafeteria; students light up with eager anticipation, which turns to disappointment if a bot does not select them. Ron turns to me.

"We should probably go check out your new dorm, Whaddya say?"

"I should go and check out this package." Naki says. "I'm so excited. Plus, classes start tomorrow."

Oh no... "You don't say?"

Seeing my alarm, Naki forms what looks like a grin.

"Don't worry Finn! If you can stand-up to Kiwok, you can handle being an Aster."

"I like the sound of that. Thanks!"

△△△

Laughing happily, our new group of friends splits up, with the trio heading off down a different hallway. Gathering my gear from Ron's room, we approach the first door on the twenty-fourth floor, 241. Ron points at the retinal scanner.

"Go ahead."

I place my right eye against the eyepiece and a blue light flashes for an instant. There is a moment's pause before the door clicks open. Ron leaps inside.

I follow right behind him. Firstly, I notice the large window directly ahead of me with black curtains drawn. The bathroom is on my left and a boot room closet on my right. Just like Ron's quarters, the bathroom has the same lemony-bleach smell and shower arrangement. A small desk is tucked in the corner beside the window. A computer with a touch-tablet and stylus rest idle. My room is exactly like Ron's. *Just cleaner.*

There is one major difference though. When I draw back the curtain from the viewport, I find that I am looking down directly over the main plaza with its incredible fountain.

On the floor is a box the length of my arm and the width of a tabletop. It's secured with a metal clasp. The Altair sigil is proudly stamped upon it. Placing my bag on the bed, I sit cross-legged on the carpeted floor. Ron joins me.

Clicking it open, I smile ear to ear.

"Wow!"

I pull out a blue long-sleeved uniform. The material looks like thick polyester but, rubbing my thumb along the front, it feels more like breathable chainmail; the back has the same silver Kraken symbol with oval-shaped eyes.

Next in the package is a sash, grey in colour and of a light material. Putting both items on the floor, I frown, eyeing up the next item in the container. It is a large contraption and I have no idea what it's for. I set it on my lap.

"What the heck is this?" I ask Ron.

"One of the most important things you'll have as a Aver," he says. "That is your Dynamic Polymer Climbing Equipment, or D.P.E for short. Ya' put that around your hips and use it to navigate harsh environments or maybe even larger enemies."

It looks like the type of object you would use to help rock climb or scale flat surfaces. It's a belt with a large front clasp. Two identical boxes containing a tiny motor are wrapped around a rope on both hips.

"Ya' know in those spy movies?" Ron says. "Where they climb up a building and stuff like that? Just aim your hip at where you want to go, press the button and boom! You're soaring like an eagle."

"Hopefully, not soaring towards my impending doom."

"Depends on the mission."

Setting the D.P.E on the carpet, I grab a set of pants and boots.

"They managed to get my shoe size?"

"Remember when ya' scanned your fingerprint at the written exams? That takes a bit of your D.N.A n' puts it in the Citadels data center."

Okay, so that means, there's no turning back...

Last, but not least, is my very own Jericho Watch. I clamp the item around my wrist as Ron stretches his arms, yawning. *Somebody needs a nap...*

Tapping the clear interface, a set of holographic

icons greets me.

"Jericho can be modified." Ron says. "Although Ulmu doesn't permit it, he can't stop a nerd from doing what nerds do."

He chuckles.

"Swipe your finger and check out the icons."

I do so. There is a section for maps, case files, study files, and when I click the last icon, a list of courses with times and room numbers appears.

"You can upload those files to your computer if you want. It's hard to read on a wristwatch."

Squinting, I scan a word. "Part...time?"

"You're a special recruit, Finn. The Citadel sought you out for the sole purpose of aiding me. You're exempt from full-time attendance. Hope ya' like homework."

He tilts his head, attempting to look at my schedule.

"Basic Weapons training, S.P.A.M, and Combat Basics?"

Ron clicks the Kraken sigil once and the hologram vanishes.

"Worry about it tomorrow; it's only three classes."

He leans on his heels.

"I'm gonna go fill out my mission report. Go ahead n' make yourself comfy. I'll see ya tomorrow."

After he's gone, I hesitantly enter the bathroom and look at myself in the mirror. Despite the spray the medic-bot put on me, tiny marks speckle my face, and my ribs throb. Getting into the shower, I let the warm water soothe away the pain.

Getting out and drying, I decide to try on my uniform. The shirt is breathable, the pants fitted with multiple pockets. Hoisting the D.P.E., I'm surprised to find that it's light as a feather. I buckle my boots which prove to be most comfortable, with soft soles. I straighten my back. *I'm an Aster now, I can do this.*

But the activities of the day have taken their toll. My gas tank is empty. I need a refuel. Flopping down on my bed, the fresh blanketing cocoons my weary bones. My head sinks into feather-down pillows. Everything goes black.

A SPIDER SHOWS ME I'M A TERRIBLE CLIMBER

Footsteps barrel towards me, instinct screams at me to wake. Enemy incoming! Is it a Spawn!? I bolt out of bed, heart pounding in my chest, a shadowy figure crosses the floor, causing the motion-triggered lights to activate.

"Ron?"

His name hisses through my clenched teeth. The blinding lights sting my eyes.

"Finn!" His voice is tinged with urgency.

"Dude, what do you want!?" I gasp.

"You're gunna be late for your first class!"

His voice hurts my head. Massaging my temples,

I try to get a grasp on what's happening. Ron flashes me his Jericho Watch.

"I was so tired after doing my paperwork. I took a nap, n' I forgot about you!" he says

"You forgot about me? Nice."

"Wait- no, that's not what I meant"

He grasps my shoulders, pulling me to my feet.

"Listen, not showing up for class when you're doing missions is fine, but you can't afford to be late on your first day."

As what he is saying sinks in, I am already on the move.

"How long do I have to get to class?"

"Uh, eight minutes!"

"Eight minutes? You must be joking!"

But I know he isn't. I'm already moving, grabbing my textbooks as Ron and I hurtle through the door into the corridor. It's a blessing I fell asleep in my uniform. It's his turn to keep up.
I don't have a chance to brush my teeth or use my deodorant. Great! Now all my fellow Asters are gunna' think humans are stupid, and stinky! My face sets into a deep frown at the thought.

An elevator arrives within moments and the doors open. I jump in. Ron stays in the corridor.

"I'm sorry but I'm gunna' have to leave you. I have my own classes to attend. All ya' gotta do is follow what's on your schedule. Got it?"

"R-right?"

What a terrible way to start my first class! I'll be starving with a caffeine headache too!

'You want Floor 442, 2B - the first door on the left side of the hall. Go get em' kid!"

The elevator doors swish closed.

"Floor 442." I command.

"442" it repeats.

We plummet, uninterrupted, to floor 442. I jump out and fling myself through the first door on the left. I find myself in a gymnasium filled with twenty Avers who are staring at me in surprise. An awkward smile twitches on my face.

"Hi."

Naki is leaning against the farthest wall. She waves at me with a smile and, as I make my way towards her, I spot Kiwok growling. I choose to ignore him as I stand beside Naki. She pats me on the shoulder.

"Nice entrance new guy."

"What did I miss?"

She giggles.

"Just the rest of the class wondering where the teacher is."

An imperious voice with a hint of disdain responds from the second gymnasium door.

"I'm right here, Miss Belle."

My Basic Weapons Instructor emerges from a door on the other side of the room from which it has, apparently, been observing its new intake.

It is, literally, a spider-like man. It strolls out with a clipboard underneath each of its spider arms. It's six feet tall, with four spider eyes and fuzzy brown skin. In its mouth are medium-sized mandibles; two horns protrude from the top of its forehead. Its greenish underbelly is partially covered by its Avers Gold uniform. Two long legs covered by boots turn to face us.

"I was waiting to see who would dare be late for my class; an apt way to wean out the weak links in my squad. Fitting that a human would be the first to disappoint."

His mandibles gnash in unison.

"Consider yourself lucky, Finn Bates. You are solely excused from classes at the grace of Godsonion Ulmu. I will ensure copious amounts of homework are forwarded to your Jericho."

Clenching my fists together, my compulsion is to scream, *don't treat me any differently from the other students!* I open my mouth but Naki grabs my wrist and shakes her head in warning. Spider-man glares at her.

"A female from Tra'vaneer in my class as well? It seems I am burdened with all the outcasts."

This time, it's gone too far. He turns his back just as I lunge forward to speak my mind. Naki puts her palm firmly on my chest and pushes me back.

"It's not worth it," she whispers.

I take a deep breath, finding my focus.

"My name is Aver Gold Socrates!" Our teacher announces. "This year, my sorry job will be to teach you pathetic lot how to use equipment vital to your survival as a Citadel armed fighting force!"

He lifts his top-right arm, triggering his Jericho Watch.

Immediately, the floor begins to tremble violently causing the majority of the Asters to go wide-eyed with fear. I see Socrates watching me and, with a considerable effort of will, I force myself to look perfectly calm. This was not what he was expecting, and I see his four eyes narrow. The challenge has been thrown down and I have accepted it.

As the rumbling continues, across the gymnasium next to the second door, a mountainous climbing wall appears. It's twenty-two feet high and pockmarked with crevices, crannies, small outcrops and toeholds. The top is framed with a fifteen-foot wide plastic pad.

Socrates's arms cross behind the small of his back.

"You will learn how to handle Photon Blasters, Plasma Blasters, the Capacitor Baton, Agron Bomb, and most importantly the Dynamic Polymer Climbing Equipment"

Socrates glares at me.

"Your D.P.E is unclipped, Finn Bates."

As I hurriedly fix the clasp, a spark of satisfaction shows in his eyes. *Guess Kiwok's not the only one I have to worry about.*

The main door whooshes open and Phender Whelcome strolls in with his webbed hands on his bulbous belly. He pauses a moment, nodding his head in Socrates's direction and addressing the class.

"Let me give you a word of advice! Don't yea' let four-eyes ruin' yer' day!"

He spots me hiding against the wall and winks.

As I smile back at him, I see Socrates' eyes narrow and the hairs on his arms raising.

"I believe you're supposed to be preparing for the advancement tests this term, Phender Whelcome, are you not?"

"Eh,' I got it all done. Go ahead. Dun' let me ruin the moment."

Socrates's lip twitches. Collecting himself, he points up at the wall.

"Four students at a time. Climb this wall. Show me what you can do. I will judge your physical abilities!"

The students are more than ready to jump to the front of the lines. Naki and I go to the back next to one another, with a couple of other "newbies" on my left. They have elongated orange faces and prehensile tails.

Naki turns to me and points to the box fixed to the D.P.E. It has three buttons. The one on the left has an arrow pointing up, the middle one has a circle and the third has an arrow pointing down. She points to the middle button with the circle.

"This one fires your hook; the arrow facing up is to climb and the arrow facing down is to reel the line back in. Press it twice to go faster."

The first four students step with their right foot

forward, aiming the corner of their hip towards the wall. They press the center button, and a thick metallic rope with a silver hook shoots from an opening.

Four hooks land on target, the students go flying through the air, landing with their feet near the top of the climbing wall. They scramble up onto the plastic pad and squat there triumphantly. Socrates claps with all four hands.

"Well done! Now, climb down by hand. Your D.P.E will not cover-up your weak skill."

The students un-clasp their hooks and reel the lines back in, climbing down by hand per Socrates's instructions. He seems pleased.

Kiwok is one of the students next in line; he fires his D.P.E. The equipment helps him up the wall, but most of Kiwok's climbing power comes from his arms and legs, which could crush boulders or snap trees in half. The equipment struggles to bear his weight, the cords twitching and groaning. He reaches the top before everybody else.

Good thing I didn't fight him in the cafeteria. He'd snap me like a glowstick.

Four more Asters of mixed species follow. Three have little trouble in completing the climb but the fourth needs two attempts which draws a sarcastic comment from Socrates.

All too soon, we are up. Despite the briefing from Naki, I get the feeling this is going to get messy. I've rock-climbed before, when I scaled the face of the cliffs around Lolly Lake, *but this isn't Lolly Lake.*

"Any day now, human!"

Maybe, I shouldn't overthink this. So, I aimlessly fire, missing the wall completely. My hook pings off the roof, clattering back down to the metal floor.

Kiwok points. "Hah!"

Whelcome sends him a death glare, the two aliens alongside us scale the wall while my face turns red. Naki appears on my left.

"Hey, Finn, just relax your core and aim with your right hip. The hook will adjust eighty degrees above you."

Socrates waves his arms dismissively.

"Climb the wall, Miss. Belle!"

Naki flashes him an eye-roll. Whelcome gets a real kick out of that, chuckling with admiration as he nods. She turns to the wall, aiming her hook, she flies forward like a comet across the night sky. Jumping over her fellow students, Naki careens over the wall onto the landing pad with graceful beauty. We stare up in amazement as I reel my anchor in.

"Impressive Miss. Belle. Your skill has surpassed my low expectations."

Socrates's compliment has a sharp edge.

I can do that too! Re-aiming, my hook lands a foot or two away from Naki's position. She stares at it wide eyed, nodding with approval.

Whelcome cheers me on.

"Good, Finn! Now just reel' yerself' in!"

Slamming my finger on the center button. The D.P.E quickly lifts me off the ground, whipping me through the air.

"Wohoo!"

The exclamation is childish, but I can't help myself. I land with both feet on the wall, my right foot slips against a cranny.

"Oh, no you don't", I tell myself.

I catch myself with my hands.

"Let go e' the wall Finn!"

Whelcome's hands form a tunnel around his lips.

"All tha' balance comes from ya' hip! Let the D.P.E do tha' work for ya'"

Despite my fear, I let go of the wall, leaning back

in mid-air. The sharp tug on my hips centers my body, keeping me upright. One tentative step at a time, I'm able to reach the top. Naki takes my hand, pulling me over the finish line.

"I guess that will have to do." Socrates exclaims sourly.

I suppose he was waiting for me to fall and hit my head.

Climbing down is easy enough, but I'm the last to land. A few of the students don't welcome my tardy pace. They roll their eyes or tap their feet.

Well, at least this won't be any different than back on earth...

We repeat the same routine a few more times and soon I'm coated in sweat. Embarrassingly, my stomach gives a loud rumble. *Hmm...food.* My concentration wavers for a moment and my foot slips off its foothold. I fall, landing butt-first on the floor. It's only a three-foot drop, but it's enough to make me go "Ouch!" and rub my tailbone. Naki helps me to my feet.

Socrates raises his arms.

"That's it for today. Now look sharp and form a line in twos"

We shuffle into a ragged formation of pairs.

Socrates is not impressed.

"Straighten up, look ahead and on the command 'quick march', leading off with the left foot – or whatever passes for one – quick march out of here. Do I make myself clear?

A reluctant chorus of "Yes, Aver." comes from our formation.

"Right, then. Quick march!"

We start to shuffle forward each at our own pace, bumping into each other.

"HALT!"

Socrates screams.

"I've never seen such a shambles. We'll keep doing this until you look like real Asters. Now, listen up! When I say 'quick march', you keep looking ahead and all move at the same pace. I will shout 'Left, Right, Left, Right,' and, as I do, you will move the appropriate appendage in time with my order. Now shape up again in a column of two, face the exit and..."

He waits until we are back in some sort of order, then yells...

"QUICK MARCH' Left, Right, Left, Right," as we make a show of marching for the first time.

Once out in the corridor, we break up into groups. I breathe a sigh of relief.

Man, am I glad to be free of Socrates' power-trip.

My glasses have slipped again. Adjusting them, I smile at Naki.

"Thank you for all the help."

"My pleasure." she pats my shoulder. Behind her a large-figure bellows.

"Aye! Kids,"

We turn to face Whelcome's outstretched arms.

"Good job today er' buddy!"

Socrates has followed us out of the gymnasium and cannot have failed to hear Whelcome's comment. Passing the various groups, he scowls and heads off away from us, clearly frustrated.

Whelcome claps his fishy hands together.

"Don't let anyone get' ye' down. Good luck, both a ye'."

He slams his palms between my shoulders, knocking the wind from my lungs.

I collect myself,

"Thanks, Phender."

Naki giggles as we wave goodbye. We go outside into the elevator corridor, wanting to escape the disapproving glares from lingering students.

"Hey, so-" I clear my throat.

Naki tilts her head with a slight look of amusement at my awkwardness.

"You're really skilled and I'm holding you back. What I mean is, I don't want that jerk, Socrates, thinking you're lame." I tell her.

Naki pauses, then laughs, fixing her head tails, so they rest properly around her ears.

"I am, in a way."

The glint in her eyes makes me realize she's waiting for me to ask the obvious question.

"I know I just met you but, why did Socrates mention your planet T'ravanner?"

I botch the pronunciation. Her bright green eyes turn sad, looking at the floor then back up at me.

"Let's just say, my species is considered to be pretty lame too."

She winks, giving me a light shove on the arm.

"We lame kids gotta stick together."

"Well, that'll be easy." I hear myself say. *Did I actually say that out loud? What will she think?!* But it does not seem to have fazed her.

"Don't be late for your next class, okay? I gotta meet up with Kisoi, I'll see you in a bit."

Naki walks off as I wave goodbye. Her natural glow is radiant, leaving me with a warm feeling in my heart.

CORPORAL VIZEN SASSES MY BULLIES

Walking over to the elevator, I head up to the dining area.

I need food...and caffeine.

The image of a hot cup of Moon-sap in my grasp as the warm steam fills my nose with a hazelnut scent is intoxicating. The cafeteria is relatively empty; I wave hello to Paypin as I walk over to the tall cylindrical container. Pressing a button, it pours Moon-sap into my Altair sigil mug.

"How was your first class?" Paypin glides over, leaving a trail of slime behind her.

"Well, let's just say I'm not dead yet."

Paypin's head swishes back and forth in approval, a bubble forms in her belly moving up to her left eye.

"Oh, I'm so happy you managed to pass. When you see Ron next, tell him he forgot to clean his plate this morning. Okay?"

She sounds happy despite the veiled threat.

"Will do, Paypin."

Sitting down in the corner, I enjoy my moon-sap, watching Altair members go about their day. Fifteen minutes pass. Raising the cup to my lips, I sip air.

I guess it's time to get back to work.

Looking down at my schedule, I frown.

Next is, Combat Basics. Great, more physical stuff. It looks like I'll be needing that medic bot again.

Combat Basics is on the four hundred and forty-second floor. As I step into the hall, I spot the gymnasium door open wide and the blue padded matting all over the floor. I'm early; only three other students are inside. They are whispering animatedly amongst themselves, lips held tight beside perked ears. Not wanting to impose, my boots pad across the matted floor as I stand on the sidelines, somewhat removed, but attempting to eavesdrop a word or two. I manage to make out a single sentence.

"Odium might be behind the attack on Othinda."

My brows furrow. I recognize Othinda as one of the four major outposts...*Is this Odium guy somebody I'll have to worry about sooner rather than later?*

Nuyen rounds the corner and her huge ice-blue eyes spot me. Before I can greet her, she lunges onto my shoulder using her claws to balance. Thankfully, the padding on my uniform saves my skin.

"Geriff! Finn. So glad to see you."

She makes a sound in her throat that is sort of like a purr, but growlier. I gather that this indicates pleasure.

"Nuyen, Hi."

I match her positive attitude.

"I missed you at Weapons Training. Aver Socrates would have been shaking in his spider-boots with you around." I smile.

Just then. Kiwok storms in and, ignoring the others, makes heads straight in our direction. Immediately, Nuyen's ears flatten against her head. Stopping beside us, Kiwok sneers contemptuously.

"Grch!, She don't gotta take weapons training. It' cause tiny' Purrinin can't wear D.P.E or use gun. She lame!"

Nuyen flashes her fangs.

"Watch it you big oaf, or I'll walk all over you!" she snarls.

It's pretty obvious that Kiwok is planning to harass us constantly and I feel anger boiling up inside me. The only way to deal with a bully is to stand up to them. I square my shoulders and, looking him straight in the face, I say in the most menacing voice I can manage…

"Leave her alone, Kiwok."

Kiwok just smiles down at me.

"Combat basics fun. Get to have training with other students. Fight really, really fun. Beat little man into ground."

He punches his fists together, then lumbers away, joining the other students as they begin stretches.

Last but not least, Naki arrives, charging towards us. Nuyen jumps off my shoulder landing in her arms.

"You're almost late, Naki."

"In your dreams." Naki teases, lifting Nuyen to her shoulder where she perches like a parrot.

Right on time, our Combat Basics teacher enters the scene.

Surprises keep coming one after another. Our teacher is a scary-looking six-foot-tall humanoid figure with a spiked carapace covering a gaping maw, exposing a double row of spiked teeth. His head is shaped like an eel, covered in white spiky plates. He has smooth skin, with patches of scales covering outer areas. A head-tail edged like a blade snakes down to his legs, moving with a mind of its own. He has purple lined markings all over his body and clawed hands. He wears the gold sash of an Aver Gold. His digitigrade legs have sharp talons at the end. He lifts his eel-shaped head, flashing two large yellow eyes at us. All in all, I am put off by his appearance.

When he speaks, however, his voice is crystal clear.

"My name is Aver Gold Vizen."

He walks on all fours, his eyes resting on Kiwok who is virtually shaking in his boots.

"I am here to ensure you are properly trained in the art of combat. Every one of you will have different strengths and weaknesses. I will teach you how to use these to your advantage against a foe.

I feel some shame at Vizen's words. *He sounds nice but I, of all people, shouldn't judge a book by its cover.*

Suddenly, Vizen jumps away from us, landing on the perimeter of the gym matting. We gasp in amazement at his agility.

"Come!" he commands. "Let's not waste time. Form a circle around the perimeter of the mats."

We do so. Naki, Nuyen and I stand next to each other. Vizen looks all of us over, head-to-toe, pausing at Kiwok.

"Claws, sharp teeth, muscle, you have many advantages, don't you, Kiwok?"

Kiwok beams with pride

"Ya' and I am son of Woya, renowned Kinquit warrior!"

Vizen's head-tail swishes through the air, he sits on his heels.

"Yes, but be careful, Kiwok. False pride is not a desirable trait for a teammate."

Kiwok scowls as Vizen continues.

"Your species, the Kinquits, are known for embarking on personal vendettas. I'm going to make sure to expose and eradicate any signs of that tendency in this unit. We cannot afford personal grudges when our lives may well depend on each other. By the time I'm finished with you, you'll be the perfect Aster."

"I'm already a perfect Aster!" Kiwok boasts.

"We'll see Kiwok. We'll see."

His voice is like ice and Kiwok is unable to look him in the eye. I have to admit that hearing Kiwok having his arrogant attitude turned against him is delightful.

Vizen makes it to Naki, and a smile forms on his mouth.

"I expect great things from you, Tra'vaneer" he says and then nods at Nuyen.

"You too, Purrinian. Congratulations on passing the exams."

Finally, Vizen comes face-to-face with me.

"Ah, the human."

His eyes scan my determined gaze; I sense him trying to discover uncertainty, but he is unsuccessful.

"I've heard much about you, Finn Bates. No claws, nor fangs- but we will find your strengths, I'm sure of it."

Vizen steps back to address us all, like a general about to lead his army into battle.

"Now, you will each, in turn step onto the mat and attack me to the best of your abilities!"

Vizen crouches on the center mat like a tiger ready to pounce.

The first Aster, armed with four horns and large hooves, hesitates before attacking Vizen.

"Come" Vizen insists. "I will not return blows; I merely wish to witness your fighting techniques."

The Aster needs no further encouragement. He charges like a bull seeing red. Vizen shifts, leaping like a frog over his back, supporting his ascent with his head-tail. The Aster turns, stunned by Vizen's agility.

"Again," Vizen commands.

The Aster kicks and Vizen ducks, skidding out of the way.

"Good, good," he says approvingly.

"Next!"

Two more students attack Vizen, but he dodges, twirling with all the grace of a ballerina.

"I'll crush you!" Kiwok brags to Vizen as the embarrassed students lumber back into the line-up.

"How confident. Come on then. Crush me"

Kiwok leaps, swinging his arms above his head. Vizen dodges to the right just as the attack brushes past his skull. Kiwok's fists thwump into the soft padding below. Vizen grabs Kiwok by the shoulders. Vaulting, he lands behind Kiwok who is swinging his arms wildly like hammers. If he managed to land a blow, he would cause serious injury but Vizen is so agile that no blow lands, maddening Kiwok even more. It is as if he is chasing a shadow.

Deciding to end the fiasco, Vizen leaps to the sidelines.

"I think I have seen enough Kinquit."

Kiwok pauses, throwing his fists in the air.

"Why can't I hit you?!" he yells.

Vizen lets a small hiss escape from his mouth.

"Not all battles need to be won, Kiwok. Please stand back in line."

Three other fights pass. Naki is soon up. Her bright emerald eyes remain keen as she stands with one hand on her hip, the other clenched at her side. Her front foot is at a twenty-degree angle.

Nuyen jumps into my arms and I struggle not to drop her.

"Naki is going to be great" Nuyen grrs. "Just watch, grr..."

Vizen is on all fours in the centre of the padded area. Naki circles him for a few moments weighing up her options. Suddenly, she aims a sideways-palm strike at his face. Vizen ducks. She raises her other palm going for an uppercut. Vizen's eyes narrow; he dodges, his legs tense, his hands reaching for her shoulders. Naki's body twists, and she grabs Vizen's wrist in a vice-like grip, pulling him around her right-side with surprising strength.

Vizen's back feet slip on the mat; Naki lifts her right leg, firing a shot into his gut. It's a light blow, but the attack resonates with the crowd causing a series of gasps and cheers. Vizen's eyes widen, seemingly appalled that one of his students was able to land a hit.

"Well done, Naki Belle-" His head-tail snaps around her ankle, throwing her to the ground. "-but not good enough."

"Augh!" she lands on her back with a heavy thump.

Vizen glides towards her.

"Very impressive, Miss. Belle! You are agile and properly trained in the art of T'ravanner combat."

He offers her his hand. She takes it, a massive smile on her face. When she returns to the lineup, we cheer.

"That was amazing, Naki."

She shrugs. "Ah, it was no big deal."

Nuyen's fur bristles with anticipation.

"Me, me!"

She runs up to the mat crouching on all fours. "Chitter, let's go, Aver, sir!"

Kiwok and the other aliens laugh. Vizen directs an icy stare in their direction and the room falls silent.

"Begin!"

To our surprise, Nuyen ducks between Vizen's legs. Using her height to her advantage, she bolts to-and-fro dodging his swiping hands. Nuyen flips, giving Vizen tiny kicks on the shins with her feet, but the paws do little-to-no damage. Her whiskers tremble in realization as her legs flex. Pouncing onto Vizen's shoulders, she fires a strike towards his head.

"Got you!"

But Vizen's head-tail lunges like a snake, wrapping around Nuyen's back paws.

"W- woah!" She exclaims as she's lifted from Vizens body and left dangling several feet off the ground like a freshly caught fish.

"Aw man." Nuyen's high pitched laughter sounds like hand-bells. "You caught me, chitter!"

Vizen's lips break into a broad smile.

"You have remarkable speed, Purrinin and you used that to your advantage. I'm impressed."

Cradling her, Vizen puts her on the ground. Nuyen bounds away, satisfied with the results.

Just me left... I'm frozen like a statue.

"Finn?"

Gulping, I step into the ring; Vizen's eyes narrow sensing my hesitation.

"Just do your best," he says quietly. "It's not a competition."

I glance at the crowd, *the look in Kiwok's eyes says differently.*

Without my move memorizer, I'm left feeling powerless. Charging forward with my fist raised, I throw a wimpish punch missing his left eye.
Vizen remains calm, circling around me. He tucks in my elbow. His skin is cold and dry.

"Arms in, core tight, swivel your hips. The strength of a punch comes from the feet, not the fists."

Glancing at the students, I see that several of

them are laughing at my humiliation. I bite my lower lip as my fists clench tighter.

Vizen's eyes thin into slits, his head spins, shooting venom in their direction.

"Enough!"

Everybody freezes.

"We, at Altair, work as a unit; we are one family, aiming to help one another grow and prosper. How do you expect to win wars with a bullish divide?! I will have no such thing in my classroom!"

The students lower their heads in shame, as my friends stare at me with familiar expressions, *pity...*

Feeling humiliated, I ask "If it's okay sir, I'd like to stand back in line."

Vizen gives a solemn nod. Returning to my friends' Naki whispers.

"You'll get better, Finn, it just takes practice."

Nuyen jumps into my arms, her thick fur blanketing my arms.

"Ya Finn, it's only day one after all."

"I suppose that's true", I admit. "All I can do is keep on trying and learning".

"That's more like it," says Nuyen. "Just one more session today, and this should be fun. We get to fly a simulator."

"A simulator?" I gasp.

"Well, of course!" says Naki. "You don't think they'd let us fly one of their fancy fighters without training, do you?

"I suppose not." I reply

"Right! Come on. The simulators are on level 447. Let's go."

We all crowd into the elevator and I feel the excitement rising. This is what we have all been looking forward to. Flying our own fighter. As the elevator comes to a halt, we spill out and head for the Training Room. Kiwok and several others have arrived ahead of us and look at us dismissively as we await the appearance of our trainer.

MY FLYING INSTRUCTOR IS A CHICKEN

Mere moments later, our teacher appears.

"Good afternoon students!"

Wait...is she a...chicken?

Not quite. She has a velociraptor-type figure, the plumage and tufts lining her body look like greenery, each different feather shades of mellowish-orange, red, and yellow. She has two peach-coloured tails flowing like ribbons as she walks. Her white eyes scan us and a smile forms on her orange beak.

"My name is Phender Liasha Lee Loreer. I will be instructing you this afternoon."

She does a quick headcount and nods in satisfaction.

"From now on, all flying instructions will be given in full flying gear! You have twenty minutes to change into full combat flying gear but, just this once, there will be qualified pilots to help you, so let's get moving!""

Loreer bolts past us and leads us to the crew room where a number of pilots, including Ron, are milling around awaiting our arrival.

"Yo' bro!" He waves and I can't help but chuckle, *talk about a coincidence.*

There are lockers all down one long wall in which hang pressure flying suits. On a shelf above them are our helmets. The sleek black and blue designs have the Altair sigil stamped on the back. These uniforms look pretty darn cool.

"When you get used to them, I expect you to get changed in 7 minutes." Loreer informs us.

"However, as this is your first time, you have twenty. The "old-timers" will help you this time. When you are ready, you will meet me in the simulator suite."

Aw man, this'll take me forever to figure out what-goes-where!

Thankfully, Ron is here to help me and I'm ready in a respectable sixteen minutes, just ahead of

Kiwok. When we finish with all the seals and tubes, we head to the simulator suite and arrive with three minutes to spare.

"Not bad, not bad at all" Loreer says. "Good, everyone's here. Now, we have 5 simulators, twenty students and 2 hours. Which means each student has 30 minutes to master the control of these fighters. Not a lot of time, you may say, but they all have A.I. and the manual and weapons controls are not complex."

She looks over the group of nonplussed students and her eyes alight on me.

"Bates, you take simulator 1 and, everyone, when you get seated, put on the helmet so that you can both hear me and speak to me."

Shocked to be her first pick, I enter the simulator cubicle, which is surprisingly compact, and settle into the pilot's seat. In front of me is a control panel with a series of switches and coloured buttons. There is a small joystick to my right-hand side.

Good thing I'm not left-handed; but, glancing down, I see that there is a socket on the floor that would allow the joystick to be switched over. The wrap-around windshield in front of me appears to be plain grey glass. *That's not going to be a lot of help.*

I put on the flight helmet as instructed. When

the other four students are in place, Loreer's voice comes over the headphones.

"In a moment, I am going to initiate the visual display and we can start to run through the controls you can see in front of you. Be ready and pay close attention. Later, you will be able to access a holographic recording of your performance that will allow you to fine-tune your responses. Righto', let's get to it!"

Immediately, the windshield becomes a 180-degree view of the launch bay, looking out into open space and twinkling stars.

"This is your view before launch. The blue switch over your head initiates the AI. You do that by flipping the switch and saying 'Prepare for launch'. Now do it."

I do so and hear a rising whine as the ion-engines start up and come up to full power.

"Systems check complete. All systems green. We are at Launch Ready."

The AI reports to me. I am more than a little nervous about what is to follow, but I am relying on my computer-gaming experience to prevent me from looking like a total moron.

Loreer demands. "Did you all get a 'Systems Green' report? Answer by numbers."

"Number 1 is green" I say.

One by one, the other four report being "Launch Ready"

"Good!" Loreer says. "Now, to the control panel, starting at the left-hand side with the switches, flip the first switch."

I do so and immediately the windshield adds a vector and ranging overlay.

"You will use this to check the location and distance of your target. This will allow you to determine which weapon you select. If the target is at some distance, you will use the propulsion-seeking argon bomb. This weapon tracks the target by its propulsion signature so that, should the target change course, the weapon will continue to home in on it. The Argon bombs are released by depressing the white button. Each ship carries 4 of these."

Loreer continues her lecture with a sense of pride.

"These can be used while you are still under AI control but for closer encounters, the AI will be switched off and you will be relying on your piloting skills and a different weapons array. We will talk more about that in the next session. For now, I want you to launch and get the feel of the joystick in controlling your flight characteristics.

To graduate from this class, you will be competing in a race to a number of designated targets and handling your craft will be critical. Good luck and tell your AI to launch."

Flying in the simulator is just like playing an arcade game, and the next thirty minutes flash by. I find that, surprisingly quickly, I'm feeling comfortable with the joystick to control the craft. The session ends when the windshield turns grey again with us all still in space but feeling exhilarated by the whole experience.

Who knew that gaming could prove so helpful in real life? And after our third session in simulation, we'll get to fly the real thing!

△△△

Our little "Losers Club" gathers together after our first session in the simulator, chattering about the experience.

Suddenly Nuyen holds up a paw, and the chatter stops.

"Who's for a moon-sap…my treat?" she asks.

Feeling in an altogether better frame of mind, we readily agree. Nuyen jumps into my arms and we all head for the elevator.

It'll be a much-needed break, after all today's crazy

classes...

Making our way to the lounge, Nuyen remains curled up in my arms.

Maybe I can convince mom to buy me a kitten for Christmas? I've never been a feline lover but having Nuyen around is oddly comforting.

"Grr, you're gonna love the lounge! It has a beautiful view, comfy couches, and it's a great place to study." Nuyen tells me excitedly.

She "grrs" again, her whiskers flicking against my palm.

"Here we are." Naki announces and leads the way into the lounge which is dominated by a window overlooking the vastness of space.

Overhanging chandeliers bathe the room with a mellow indigo hue. Turquoise couches with black leather trim wrap around the walls. Coffee tables made from a silver material glimmer and gleam. Five Asters are in the room, taking up the far-left couch facing the right window. Other aliens occupy many of the other tables and the room is alive with an excited buzz of chatter and alien "laughter".

Naki weaves her way forward towards a set of stairs that I have not noticed until now. They lead to a lower level. We follow her down and I find myself in an area that is comfortably set up, with oval-shaped, softly cushioned seats that allow a spectacular view of space through the large windows that form the exterior wall. The lighting is soft and the atmosphere quieter. *I love it.*

"Best seats in the house." Naki says with pride.

We all sit in a semicircle. Nuyen remains in my lap and I instinctively gently scratch her head. She "grrs" with pleasure, and her tail swishes back and forth.

Naki taps her Jericho Watch, typing in a message with a small holographic keypad.

"What are you doing?" Nuyen asks.

"Telling Kisoi where we are. He should be done with his Planetary Studies by now."

Her brother arrives a few moments later, with Ron in tow. Kisoi sits next to his sister, giving me a wave.

"Nice to see you again, Finn."

I aim to reply, but my boorish brother cuts me off.

"Yo' dude!"

Ron plops down on my right side and puts his feet up onto the coffee table.

"How are those classes going for ya'?" he asks me.

I look pointedly at his boots and glare, but he doesn't take the hint.

"I would say not bad, but Socrates got mad at me for being late."

My brother waves his hand dismissively.

"Hey, don't worry about that four-armed jerk. You can skip his class all ya' like."

Naki shakes her head in disagreement.

"No offence, Ron; that might have worked for you when you were an Aster Bronze, but the same won't apply for Finn. No way he'll pass with Socrates hating him"

"Psh!" Ron shrugs. "That spider is a total jerk."

Ron turns to me.

"Don't listen to anything he says. You got Ulmu on your side."

Admittedly, I'm opposed to the idea of breaking the rules just because the Godsonion likes me, but...

"Trust me bro. Listen to Phender Whelcome. He's the only sane teacher 'round here."

Kisoi chimes softly.

"I suppose, but surely that's up to Finn?"

"I'll be alright," I chuckle. "Apart from him,

classes went well. Aver Vizen is my favourite although; and the simulator session was terrific."

Nuyen yawns.

"Vizen's weird, but he yells at Kiwok, so that's good."

Her large blue eyes narrow and she catapults from my lap, nudging Ron's boot with her claws.

"Whaddya want?" Ron exclaims.

"Listen Mr. Aver Bronze, First Class! Show some manners! Get your feet off the table, mahrrr!"

Ron shrugs, removing his dirty boots from the previously clean tabletop. He adopts a seductive tone.

"How can I say no to somebody as cute n' fuzzy as you?"

Nuyen sticks her tongue out playfully.

"Keep the compliments coming, mister!"

I need to cut in, before the bantering gets out of hand.

"Hey, Ron. Where have you been anyway?"

My brother turns to me, crossing his legs, specks of dirt falling to the floor.

"I take classes too ya' know. Advanced Combat, Advanced tactics and Strategy plus Planet Studies. Ulmu is makin' me. He said, 'Sorry Ron, you won't graduate to Aver Gold if you don't learn your planets!'"

Kisoi laughs.

"It's kinda true, though. You can't pass if you're napping in class all the time."

Ron raises a finger, as if he is about to argue Kisoi's point, then he shrugs, slumping into his chair.

"What do you study, Kisoi?" Ron asks.

"Mainly, F.S.K.A.'

Kisoi sees my puzzled look.

"Sorry, Finn. That's 'Foreign Species Knowledge and Application'. I guess I'm kinda' a bookworm."

"Every team's gotta have one." Ron grins.

Kisoi's eyes sparkle with gratitude and a massive smile forms on his face. Moving on, we chat about how we arrived on Altair.

"We're from the planet T'ravannerr-" Kisoi tells me. "Many of our people are training at the Othinda outpost. So, what about you, Finn?"

"I'm nothing special."

Kisoi tilts his head, eyes darting questioningly towards Ron who shrugs.

"Our parents live back on Earth, in a small town named Baysite Heights." he says. "It's real' cute."

Ron smiles as the memories form in his mind.

That's right...Ron doesn't know about mom and dad's divorce.

My neck and back stiffen at the realization. Thankfully, my elder brother is too busy reminiscing to notice my discomfort.

"Dad travels and mom's a waitress. I'm aiming to see em' again real soon."

Ron looks at me, his large brown eyes filled with hope. I blink, forcing a small smile to form on my lips. Kisoi and Naki glance at one another, then back at us.

Kisoi affectionately comments.

"Ron, if the majority of humans are like you, I'm sure you'll prove that Earth deserves to be a Known planet."

He turns to me.

"You, too, Finn."

RON AND I HAVE A DEATH-DEFYING SPACE RACE

The next few weeks pass in a blur. We seem to be on an accelerated course and, with much of the learning to be done by studying in the evenings, we don't get much time to socialize. However, our little group does get together each morning for breakfast and Ron joins us occasionally.

Towards the end of the sixth week, we are having breakfast, and Ron is sitting with us. We are all excited as this is the morning that we are being tested on our flying abilities with the fifteen-target challenge.

Nuyen glances at her watch.

"Come on," she says. "We don't want to be late for this session. It's gonna be wild!"

We get up to head for the elevator. Kisoi and Ron get up and join us.

"Wait," I say. "Are you guys coming with us?"

Ron gives me a thumbs up.

"You didn't know? It's tradition to have volunteers from higher ranks race against the new students. It aids Loreer in assessing the new students' skill level; we also watch out for you, just in case something happens."

Ron jokes as the elevator door opens.

"Like, if your spacecraft explodes, boom!"

He makes an exploding gesture with his hands; I nudge him with my shoulder.

"Come on; I'm already freaked out."

Naki prods her elbow against mine.

"Don't worry; it's not as difficult as it sounds."

An uncomfortable silence follows as we enter the immense launch bay 1B, which is holding a large number of single-pilot ships decorated in Altair colours. They all have the Kraken sigil on the nose and bodies; their wings are folded into the sides of the hulls. Seen through the clear windshields is one single black seat surrounded by the now-familiar control panels and switches.

We join the rest of the class. Kiwok looks to be in a sour mood as usual. The other Fledgils stand in a group gaping at a row of twenty gleaming fighters, each facing a closed launch portal.

Ron is standing, grinning with the other Aver Bronze pilots against whom we will be competing. As one, they file out through a door at one end of the hangar.

Loreer appears through a door at the back of the launch deck.

"Righto' everyone. Today you will be graded on what you have learned over the past six weeks. The Aver Golds that will be paired off with you will perform a synchronized launch from Deck 1A."

She flaps her wings in excitement.

"As you have learned, this is a race! There are fifteen hoops positioned at coordinates pre-loaded into your nav system. They will take you to a point 65 clicks from each target. Your challenge is to fly your ship through each hoop. Miss one, and you fail. And, by the way, the hoop is designed to only allow one ship at a time through it. Time to fly."

She leads us to the stunning row of fighter jets. They are all finished in a non-reflective black coating with only a small Kraken sigil on their side to identify them as Citadel craft. There is also a symbol which translates to a number so that pilots can identify each other in battle.

"These are from the brand-spankin' new Comet Series!" Loreer says proudly.

We stand, gaping, awaiting her instructions. She snaps her beak again.

"Hurry up! Pick your fighter."

"Me, first!" Kiwok yells and starts to move towards the first craft. Loreer's sharp voice brings him to a swift halt.

"Not that first aircraft, Kiwok. You get number two. The seat is lower and wider to accommodate your size. The rest of you take your pick."

As the flood of students race towards the closest ships, my legs freeze. I try to kick them into gear, but they refuse to respond.

Nuyen pads across the floor fast as lighting, pursued by Naki, her head-tails bounding behind her and soon all the aircrafts have a student standing beside them…all that is except for the machine at the end of the line, which looks subtly different.

It has a cylindrically shaped body with a rounded nose. Its bodywork leaves a lot to be desired, and its colours range from baby-blue to dull-grey.

The wings are entirely retracted into the fuselage.

Loreer appears beside me, her beak inches away from my ear.

"Hm, it appears we are one jet short, so you'll be flying the older Moon series 200 model!"

She points to the ship at the end of the line. The rest of the students look at my dilapidated ship, snickering. *Can't they leave me alone for two seconds?*

Naki and Nuyen are glaring at Kiwok who can't hold back his contempt.

"Stop laughing, you lug!" Naki snaps, but Kiwok shrugs.

Loreer is oblivious to what's happening around her and walks with me to my ship.

"The best ships are those with personality, Finn." She says. "I rode the Comet Series 200 for years and I'm not dead yet! You'll be fine!""

I give her a half-hearted grin and peer into the cockpit, studying the controls. *Is that blue tape on the joystick?*

I am about to ask her why but she is already on her way back to address the higher-ups.

"Alrighty students, synchronize your Jericho

Watches, and code them to open the cockpits!"

We do as she says, and the cockpit covers glide back. As soon as they open, the students eagerly clamber aboard and are settling themselves into their seats. The more experienced pilots are already strapping themselves in.

My cockpit cover remains stubbornly closed. Loreer hurries over to me.

"Don't tell me! You're the slowpoke."

"I coded like everyone else, but nothing has happened." I explain.

"Oh, son of a..." she swears. "I'm so sorry, Finn. That's my fault. This older model uses a different code. Here, give me your watch."

She takes it from me, recodes it and, immediately, my cockpit opens. It doesn't slide back like the others, however. It hinges up.

Feeling a little less like an idiot, I jump in...*last again!*

I find the seat adjustment control and use it to set the seat in the most comfortable position for my frame. On close inspection, I'm not sure why there is blue tape on the joystick flight control and I'm not going to remove it to find out.

There is no conventional control panel, as you might see on a commercial jet on Earth. This is equipped with a full heads-up display on the windshield such as modern fighters have, but much easier to read. Tentatively moving the joystick, I realize that it controls all aspects of the fighter's attitude and appears to handle like the vessels I have been flying on the simulator.

Finally, something that feels familiar! No wonder Ron said that it was like playing Galaga.

I feel a measure of confidence returning. I'm considered to be pretty good at the game. *This might actually end up being a chance to demonstrate that I am not a total loser.*

That's when I spot a red button with a flame sticker inches away from my left foot. I call over to Loreer.

"Aver Loreer? What is this butto..."

But she is preoccupied and is back at the head of the line.

"Ok, now close up your cockpits! I will be monitoring you from the Traffic Control Suite throughout this exercise. Stay alert and listen carefully to your fellow pilots and to my voice when it is needed."

Almost as one, the cockpit covers on the other jets slide closed. It takes me a moment longer to work out how to make my cover swing down and lock.

"Check your pressure seals, by number," she orders.

"One is green."

"Two is green". Kiwok's voice is unmistakable.

"Three is green."

One by one, the other sixteen fighters check in, which ensures that by the time it gets to me, I am ready to report...

"Twenty is green."

Loreer's voice comes over the headphones.

"Students, your Flight Designation is 'Aqua'. Avers, yours is Turquoise. Ron, as exercise commander, you are Turquoise one, Finn, you are Aqua 20. Make sure you all know your number. It will also show up in the top left-hand corner of your heads-up display. I will be pairing you at random from Traffic Control. Good luck and fly safely."

She disappears through a steel door at the end of the hangar and up to the Traffic Control Suite. A few moments later, her voice comes over our headphones.

"As this is a simulated emergency scramble, engine-start permission is granted to all."

I order the AI to start the ignition sequence and,

in moments, forty ion-rocket engines fire up as all craft prepare for departure. They are surprisingly quiet but immensely powerful.

"Hello." a robotic male voice sounds through my headphones.

There are two communication channels available. Aircraft to aircraft and aircraft to Control, and this is neither.

"Ship examination complete. All systems online. Moon Series 200 ready for take-off."

Realization hits me; *He's the Moon Series AI for this particular aircraft so he is automatically connected solely to me, as the pilot.*

Loreer's voice cuts through this realization.

"Airlock is cycling for launch. Each pair will launch simultaneously at three-minute intervals. The first pair will be Turquoise 7 versus Aqua 12. The last pair will be Turquoise I and Aqua 20. A little brotherly competition should make for some excitement. First pair, acknowledge."

"Turquoise 7 acknowledged."

"Aqua 12 acknowledged."

I sit there watching pair after pair launch with the tension rising during the hour between the first launch and ours. Loreer is watching each pair closely from Traffic control. Finally, Loreer's voice comes over our headphones.

"Turquoise 1 and Aqua 20 acknowledge."

Immediately, I hear Ron's voice.

"Turquoise 1 acknowledged."

"Aqua 20, acknowledged."

My voice sounds half an octave higher than usual. Ron calls me on the ship to ship link.

"Getting nervous, Bro'?"

"No...just looking forward to kicking your ass."

I hear him laugh as the launch countdown begins.

My grip tightens on the throttle. The heads-up display comes to life, casting shadows up my face. The engines create a soft whining sound behind me. Now that it is actually time to fly this thing, and without consciously being aware of it, my gaming experience asserts itself as I gently ease the throttle open. As we begin the roll-out, the wings that have been tightly closed now sweep out in a familiar delta formation.

I decide to address the A.I.

"Moon Series 200?"

"How can I help you?" The voice sizzles and pops.

"What is this red button on the floor?"

"That is a turbo boost installed by the previous owner. Probability of foreign object complying with Moon Series 200's internal components is 45.07%."

"Meaning?"

"It would probably be inadvisable to push that button as it has slightly less than a 50% chance of being compatible with this craft."

Clearly, this AI has a dry sense of humour. Once clear of the launch bay, I push the throttle halfway open.

Woah! The rate of acceleration causes my stomach to flip and my body is pressed back into my seat.

"Would you like to engage in mirror mode?" the AI asks.

Without thinking it through, I pump my fist.

"Heck ya."

Four projectors light up against the window of my cockpit. One shows me a view to the right of the ship. The second shows the left side. The third is an enhanced view ahead with vectors and ranges indicated. The fourth view appears to be from the underbelly of the craft and points back to where Altair H.Q. is a distant metal-marble that quickly disappears from view.

"Turquoise 1, you should now have the obstacle course on visual," Loreer informs us about seven minutes later.

"Flight Control, Turquoise One. Obstacle course in sight." Ron replies

In the far distance, I see a floating ring painted the typical Altair blue. My long-range display shows that it is the first of the fifteen that are arranged in a U shape, the tail end of the course hundreds of miles away but having us heading back towards Altair.

Ron and I have maxed out our throttles and are virtually side-by-side as we approach the first ring. As we close with it, neither of us seems willing to back off.

"Ron, we won't fit." I call to him.

"So, chicken out!" he replies.

Growling, I slacken off a fraction, stopping us from colliding. I sail through the ring immediately behind him. The AI link to the navigation computer vectors us towards the second ring several clicks away. Shoving my whole body on the acceleration throttle, I jerk forward scuttling ahead of Ron just as we hit the next loop.

Our ships veer again as the nav system swings

us towards the third hoop and, once again, Ron whips through it at full throttle with me a mere second behind. I make the fourth hoop a fraction ahead of him and this cat and mouse contest continues for the next 9 rings. The fifteenth and final ring is now about three minutes away and Ron is just ahead of me.

That's when I remember the red button beside my foot.

"Moon Series 200, what was that probability of success if I use the booster?"

"45.07%."

"Well, today, I'm feeling lucky."

Like the semi-moron I am, I slam my boot on the button.

BOOM! A halo of quivering particles burst from my thrusters. The surge of acceleration pushes me back into my seat. The stars rush by as I fight to maintain control.

"Maximum velocity." the AI informs me. I realize that I am now closing the distance with Ron's ship and I'm not quite at full throttle. Next thing, I am alongside him.

"I told you I'd kick your butt," I tell him.

"As if-" Ron snaps. "-I'll never lose against an Aster!"

Ron clearly doesn't understand how important it is for me to win! *Plus, I want to see Kiwok's face when the human kid beats an Aver Bronze in a space race!*

"You think?" I say. "Watch this." Jerking the joystick hard left, the world spins one-hundred and eighty degrees and I fly, inverted, directly above him.

Positioned upside down above Ron's ship, blood rushes to my face, my hair hangs freely.

"Uhm, Bates brothers,"

Loreer's voice comes over our headphones.

"Let's not kill each other, shall we? You are expendable but those ships are expensive!"

Too little too late, brushing off her genuine concern, we fly at max velocity, the finish line getting closer. My ship is a hurricane, Ron's, a tornado. The finish line is less than a mile away from destruction.

Now!

Slamming my Jericho Watch, the ship shuts down; the control panel flickers, then fades, as I continue to rush forward due to the now maxed-out momentum created from the turbo boost. Anti-gravity hits, causing me to float against my seat.

"What the...?" Ron's alarmed voice cries.

I am speeding towards the last hoop upside down and at a downwards angle. Had the wings still been deployed, I would have smashed them against the hoop but, as it is, I have enough clearance to speed across the finish line like a bullet, leaving Ron inches behind.

As soon as I am through, I reactivate the AI and then perform the traditional victory roll before ordering the AI to trim the ship for landing.

"Unbelievable, Finn!" Lorreer calls. "Well done."

Within minutes, the AI has us both back in the Launch Bay. I climb out of my ship to the cheers and hollers of the other students. Naki waves, with her cheeks flushed, Kisoi seems filled with pride.

Moments later, Ron arrives from the deck above. He comes straight over to me and claps me on the shoulder, shaking his head in disbelief.

"Well done, bro! See? I knew you could do it. You just needed a little push."

"A little?" I argue. "You almost killed me."

"But are you dead?" he shrugs. Despite my attempts to be cool about the win, my heart is filled with joy.

*Just one thing left to do...*I climb the steps up to the cockpit, lean in and reactivate the AI.

"How may I help you?" it asks.

"Thanks for the help, Moon Series 200."

"My pleasure," he replies.

"You know, calling you by your model is a mouthful,"

I remember the nickname Ron has for Eunoia.

"How about I call you, Luna? That means moon in Latin."

"Noted!"

Luna chimes.

"From now on, all ship functions will respond to the nickname, Luna."

I TAKE A ROAD TRIP TO CREYENIA

Loreer guides us back to a crew area.

The class has concluded, and we end on a high note. My friends are all talking about my terrific maneuvering as we gather in a group. Kisoi pats my back.

"That was amazing, Finn, shutting down your ship. How did you think of that?"

"Instinct I guess."

The grin on my face says otherwise.

Ron moves to stand beside me.

"As I said," he gloats. "You just needed the right motivation."

"Motivation?" I say in disbelief. "Looked like you just wanted to win"

Ron shrugs,

"Like good ol' times!" The memories flood back and ease the tension from my face. "But listen mister high n' mighty, round two will be different."

We are standing side-by-side when Ron's Jericho Watch lights up. He unlocks the screen, swiping to a notification symbol.

Ron's face lights with unmistakable delight.

"What does it say?" Kisoi asks.

Ron turns towards me.

"Guess what? We've got a mission."

Naki crosses her arms, leaning against the elevator wall.

"Guess Ulmu wants to test you out on the battlefield."

She sounds sombre. *Looks like she wants her own mission.* Kisoi taps me on the shoulder, drawing my attention away from Naki.

"It's okay, Finn." He insists. "We're rooting for both of you."

Nuyen springs up into Naki's arms, managing a supportive smile.

"That's right, good luck, grr!"

Ron and I enter the elevator, parting ways with the Losers' Club. Once the elevator doors close, Ron pumps his fists, smiling like a mad man.

"I can't wait to see what Ulmu's got for us! Maybe it's a murder mystery or a political scandal?"

His imagination runs wild.

"Ooh, or a foreign alien invasion on a civil Known Planet!"

"I'm not sure I'm ready for that."

He shoves me, sending me stumbling into the wall.

"You've got **me**! No matter what, I'll make sure ya' live."

That coming from the guy who would have blown our ships to smithereens during our race. I'll assume I need to rely on my own brains most of the time, not that Ron's abundance of enthusiasm isn't welcome.

We reach the top level, the elevator doors whoosh open and Ron beelines into Ulmu's office. I follow and we stand at attention while Ulmu types on his holographic keyboard. As soon as he sees us, he smiles.

"Stand easy gentlemen. I hear that you two you had an exciting race today. Congratulations Finn. A neat manoeuvre."

"Thank you, sir" I grin.

"Right then. Now, please be seated."

We sit in the comfortable guest chairs.

He immediately leans into his desk, retrieving a small oblong box. He stands, comes to where I am sitting and hands me the box.

"You may find these useful" he says with a smile.

Carefully, I pry the box open.

"My glasses?" *No, something is different.* The rims are thicker, with a slight pearl-grey and navy trim. Beside the right hinge is a button. Ulmu nods.

"I figured you'd need these. Take care of them"

He goes back behind his desk and leans across it.

"And don't lose them."

Looking at Ron for guidance, he furrows his brow, shrugging. Gingerly I slide the glasses up my nose and am fascinated when the lenses light up neon- blue. A line of text reads *"Move Memorizor Interface, Initiated."*

"No way..." my hand covers my shocked expression. Ulmu winks with his two left eyes.

"I had your Drakkinion friend assist in the modifications. I think we will keep this particular undertaking secret."

"Y- yes, sir."

The lenses fade to clear and are adjusted to the strength of my old pair.

"This is amazing."

A squeaking sound comes from Ron's chair as he leans back.

"If they had laser beams, that woulda' been way cooler."

Ulmu shakes his head, smiling.

"I ordered you two here to give you the details of your mission."

Ron leans forward again, quickly placing his elbows on his knees and rubbing his hands greedily, like a child eager for a treat.

"Your mission is located at map marker K-A-2022, the planet Creyenia."

Ulmu knits his hands together.

"It is a planet inhabited by the Ghahlaous, peaceful shadow people settled in the dense forests of Creyenia."

The description calls up strange imagery of haunted woodlands filled with ghost-like aliens.

"The Ghahlaous worship a sort of god-tree

named Gaaqet who, for hundreds of years, has populated them with new beings at the end of every moon cycle" he continues. "Rather like a tree shedding seeds, you could say. Recently, however, the tree has grown sickly and has stopped creating populace. Unless the Ghahlaous find an answer, they are facing extinction. Your job is to examine the tree, then relay your findings back to Altair so that we may look for a cure. Any further details we may acquire will be sent to your Jericho Watches".

"This is simply a relay mission?"

Ron rolls his eyes, but Ulmu remains patient.

"Ron, you may be capable of completing high-ranking missions, but your brother needs experience. A mission like this is a good first step, requiring, as it does, diplomacy...not your strongest characteristic."

He waves his hand dismissively.

"Now, no more complaining. You will leave immediately. I have instructed Loreer to transport Finn's battleship onto Eunoia. This mission shouldn't take longer than two or three days. Understood?"

My back straightens. "Yes, sir."

Ron shrugs, a coy grin on his face.

"Cool beans."

"Now go, and good luck."

△△△

Arriving at the launch bay, I am once again impressed with Eunoia's size. She is massive, especially considering she will have a crew of just two. My Moon Series 200, "Luna" and Ron's Comet Series 300 are being loaded and locked into position through the ships launch portals.

"I don't know why they're bothering. We're not likely to need them."

"Don't look so glum." I tell him. "This is my first mission. Did you really expect to be sent on a murder mystery?"

Ron rolls his shoulders, letting loose a huge yawn.

"When you say it like that, I guess not. I just get so bored."

Boarding, our boots clank against the loading bay as Euonia's launch portals close.

"Ya' better be a fast learner, bro. We have a long way to go before earth becomes a Known Planet."

I pass in front of him, into the airlock.

"Let's take our time Ron. Slow and steady wins the race."

Once the airlock is secure, we stand in the crew lounge. Ron gestures towards the far wall.

"I added your I.D. to the weapons locker. Go ahead n' grab your equipment."

I walk across to the locker and use the retinal scanner for access. I grab a plasma pistol, folding it into a square, and a Photon Blaster along with a leg holster and leg pouch which I put on. The Photon Blaster is now nestled against my left leg. Looking down at the Argon Bombs, I grimace. *Too much? Or not enough?* I grip two of them, placing them in my pouch. *Please. Don't blow my leg to smithereens.* I metaphorically knock-on-wood.

Now that I am armed, we head straight up to the flight deck. My fingers lace around the metal bars lifting me up the ladder. I jump into the co-pilot's seat and ensure that my safety harness is locked. I spot my reflection in the windshield. There are dark circles under my eyes, and below are small cuts on my upper lip.

Ron takes his place in the pilot's seat, straps in and activates EON.

"Eunoia, case file Ghahlaous, insert coordinates."

"Coordinates assessed. K-A-2022."

Eunoia gives a gentle shake preparing for launch.

Ron takes us up rough and choppy, leaving Altair behind in the distance. Boosting into space, he blasts Eunoia into hyperdrive. Inside a flash of brilliant white light, we zoom through the cosmos at light-speed.

Ron studies me and grins.

"So, whatcha think about Naki?" *Oh no...*

I shrug.

"She's nice, but so are Nuyen and Kisoi."

He smiles ear to ear. I point an accusatory finger.

"No, Ron, don't do this again."

"Again?"

"Back when we were in school, you always tried to pair me with other girls in my class. Not. Interested."

"All boys are interested in girls! Well, most of 'em!"

He attempts to hold back his laugh. I know he can sense the conversation bothers me.

"Listen, little bro, I know you ain't ever been on a solid date."

"How would you know? You disappeared for five

years, remember?"

"I can tell by the blush on your cheeks."

"Jerk."

He finally bursts out into laughter.

"If you want first-date recommendations, hit me up. I know everything there's to know about ladies!"

He thumps his chest in a congratulatory manner.

"You think you're a lady's man?" I ask.

"Sure am, dude."

Looking back at him with an evil gleam in my eyes, a memory floods in.

"What about when you sneezed into that girl's soda cup on your first date to the movie theatre?"

Ron's eyes go wide, his lips tighten, and he crosses his arms.

"Trust you to remember that. Her name was Samantha, and that never happened."

"So you say!" I grin.

There is no time left for joshing each other as we burst out of hyperdrive. Ron's Jericho Watch immediately starts flashing, warning of an incoming message. Ron accesses it and scans it.

"What?" I ask

"Well, it's not good news. Apparently, this place has an unbreathable atmosphere. We'll have to suit up.

He looks up from his watch.

"Oh, jeez! Look at that." He exclaims

I look ahead and, on the horizon, a shocking view wipes the grin off my face.

Creyenia circles around three identical silver moons. Pallid, dark-gray clouds loom over shadowy treetops. Light years away, a red giant blasts scorching-hot rays of light across the misty topography. As Ron takes us down into the atmosphere, our windshield fogs up and droplets of rain hamper our vision. Ron uses Eunoia's surprisingly effective air blasters to clear the raindrops away. Dipping into the lush forest, darkness overtakes us.

"Creepy..."

A shiver trickles up my spine. Ron takes over the controls from EON and sets us down carefully. He tells EON to close down and Eunoia's engines go silent.

"I assume we aren't getting a formal greeting?" he says.

"Maybe we won't meet anybody?"

"Alrighty, let's haul off." Ron declares.

He stands, taking a moment to stretch. He looks at me, still sitting in my seat.

"Come on, up n' at 'em. Time to suit up."

He starts off down the ladder. Following him down to the crew deck, I stick the white sash in a loop. We draw spacesuits from their storage locker and climb into them. We then arrange our weapons for quick access, and I struggle with adjusting my D.P.E. to ease the pressure on my back.

"Do you guys have chiropractors on Altair?" I ask.

"Nope, but I'm sure Miv can crack yer' limbs like a glowstick."

Ron opens the inside door of the airlock. We squeeze in, the door closes behind us and the airlock cycles. As soon as it finishes, Ron opens the outer hatch and the ramp glides out.

We step onto Crevenian soil and Ron closes the entry hatch. Looking out, the darkness of the forest is instantly disturbing, and I feel a twinge of fear in my gut. The tree branches are like hands clawing at the sky. I can envision them scratching my face, trying to gouge my eyes out.

Stepping into the damp air, each step is harder to

take than the last. Looking down, I see that the ground is soft and mushy all around us. Beneath the thick moss, I hear the smoosh of wet dirt and rainwater. Ron shields his eyes with his left hand staring up at the cloudy sky.

"Shoulda' brought a raincoat. Next time, remind me to check the weather network before landing on an alien planet."

Suddenly, we hear branches crack. The bushes rustle.

"Death to the intruders!!"

That doesn't sound good.

Reaching into my back pocket, I arm myself with the plasma pistol, triggering its transformation from hilt to handle. Quick as lighting I aim at a pair of heads. Ron steps forward, his hand lingering against his holsters.

Two medium-sized shadow figures, dressed in primitive armour made from wood, burst from the tree-line, bearing wooden spears tipped with polished stone. The pointed ends are aimed towards us. They remain calm like seasoned hunters.

"We're from Altair." Ron calls. "We're the Citadel members sent to examine the Tree. We're here to help you."

Ron lowers his gun.

"See? Friends."

The Ghahlaous lower their spears. They have humanoid bodies made entirely from swirling mist. The tops of their heads flicker like smoke curling from a burning fire. One of the men sighs, his white eyes staring at both of us.

"We have never seen your kind before. What is your purpose here?"

"My name is Ron Bates, I'm a human from Planet Earth, and an Aver Bronze from the Citadel's Altair outpost. This is Finn Bates, an Aster Bronze."

The Ghahlaous on the right glares at us.

"These words mean nothing to us. How are you to help us?"

Ron steps forward, placing his hands on his hips.

"We were informed that Gaaqet is dying, right?"

The two Ghahlaous men seem perturbed.

"This is a simple relay mission." Ron says.

"Gamirah..." a new name "She must have..."

The Ghahlaous pauses.

"Come with us. Our elder will explain further."

With that, we strike out into the forest, leaving

Eunoia and the safety of our ship behind. We stick close to them as they push away looming foliage and sharp branches.

Ron jabs my shoulder.

"Call me crazy, but I don't think this is going to be a relay mission."

"I caught onto that too." I tell him. "Should we turn back, do you think?"

"Heck, no dude, this is our chance to show Ulmu we can handle larger missions."

"Sounds reckless." I venture.

"Reckless is just another word for fun." he replies.

For three minutes, we plow through the unforgiving terrain before breaking into a clearing. Rows of thick trees border a flattened path on the further side.

"This is our capital, Girah." Our guide says. "When the god-tree, Gaaqet, gifts us with new lives, many come here to spend their remaining years in peace, until we eventually fade, returning to the stars."

He looks at the sky longingly.

"Inside these trees, we nest, spending the long nights sharing tree bark, and protecting our own. Now that we have recently become a

Known planet, your Citadel offers us new knowledge and protection."

The soldier bows his head, a small gesture of appreciation. He turns on his heels to guide us through Girah.

The homes of the Ghahlaous are in the trees and are accessed by wooden staircases that climb up to the branches. I'm enamoured by the beautiful fairy lights tied along rope-bridges connecting their homes. Bundles of soft grass are beautifully decorated into dens. It appears that most Ghahlaous sleep on moss beds, sharing bark, eating the plantation like beef jerky. They look happy, talking in a foreign language that gets roughly translated by my earpiece.

"Our elder, Girit and her apprentice Gamirah live here."

Our guide gestures to the largest oak tree with his spear.

"They will not have been expecting you."

One of the two guards goes ahead to announce and then returns.

"Girit will see you." He tells us and then he and his companion walk away, holding their weapons high and proud.

The opening to Girit's abode is carved by hand

from the wood of a large branch that grows across the entrance. Another Ghahlaous is standing beside the fabric-covered doorway and greets us as we enter. She is a female, judging by her long hair whips cascading down the nape of her neck. She's wearing a flowing summer-type dress fashioned with large leaves and vines. Her facial features are dark like the others, but her large, twinkling, silver eyes show childish wonder. A smile forms on her grey lips and, in her arms, she holds a number of Citadel sanctioned books.

"So happy that you are here to help us!" she chimes.

She places the books on the moss bed and grabs my hand in an awkward shake.

"My name is Gamirah. I'm Girit's apprentice and the first Ghahlaous'e to learn Citadel tech; I'm considered to be kinda' a genius. I'm almost thought of a god myself, which is fun. Anyway, cool outfits. You guys look armed to the teeth!"

While she rambles, Gamirah doesn't unhand me. Her skin is colder than the peak of Mount Everest. I grit my teeth against the pain.

"N- nice to meet you Gamirah. My name is Finn."

She finally let's go, shaking Ron's hand.

"My name is Ron."

I notice that he gets goosebumps on his arms. When she releases his hand, he rubs the warmth back.

"Ron and Finn,...super-duper cool names!"

A new voice speaks, deep and raspy, from behind a curtain at the back of the entranceway.

"Down, Gamirah. We have serious matters to attend to. I'm sure these men don't want their ears talked off."

I smile at Gamirah, who pouts and picks up her books again, hugging them to her chest.

"I- I don't mind," I tell the mysterious voice emanating from the hidden room behind the drape.

Ron rolls his eyes. Gamirah turns, leading us past the drapes. Inside, the Ghahlaous elder sits, cross-legged, on a flower bed.
Girit has a wooden walking cane and a hunched back. She is many feet shorter than Ron. Her wispy hair flows down to her knees.

"I am Girit, the eldest Ghahlaous'e on Creyenia."

She gives a simple head nod to Gamirah who quickly sits beside her.

"Please sit." She says and we sit on the soft moss also. I rest my hands firmly in my lap.

"I told Gamirah to send a request to the Citadel

for advice about our current problem. I was not expecting them to send you here to help us."

Ron flashes a startled look.

"I'm sorry elder Girit, but we were ordered simply to examine Gaaqet and report our findings in order that we might find a treatment. Your apprentice said that she was glad that we were here to help you, which makes it sound as if you are expecting something more?"

Gamirah stares into the distance, Girit shoots a harsh glare her way, causing the young apprentice to flinch.

"Gamirah," the elder demands, "What exactly did you message the Citadel?"

Gamirah's dark lips tighten into a frown.

"You know we couldn't afford to tell them the whole truth. So, I might have underestimated our predicament."

"You lied?" the elder snaps.

"But elder Girit, if we'd told them about the murders, we wouldn't be able to afford their support!"

Afford our support? I thought the Citadel willingly helped Known Planets out as one of the benefits of membership.

"I don't understand." I said.

I gesture to Ron, who has an uptight look on his face.

"What do you two mean you couldn't afford to tell the truth?"

Ron looks uncomfortable.

"I should have told you bro', but I just knew it woulda' left a bad taste in your mouth. The Citadel has to pay us somehow, in Galaxy Coins."

"And we extract that money from struggling people?"

An edge of poison seeps into my words. Girit raises her wooden staff waving it.

"We understand the importance of the Citadel. We offer payments as best we can. Unfortunately, the more difficult our problems, the more the Citadel charges. It seems young Gamirah knew our funds were running short and informed The Citadel that our predicament was a simple relay mission."

"When, in fact, it's not?"

Now it is Elder Girit who looks uncomfortable.

"No." she replies sadly. "Not if you are to help us. Gaaqet is, in fact, sick, but, more worrying, members of our community are also missing. We sent the bulk of our male militia to investigate and they have not returned."

Gamirah pleads.

"We think Gaaqet has gone mad. If we told the Citadel this, they would send an experienced platoon. We can't afford that."

She bows, looking up at us with eyes full of hope.

"Please, help us."

I want to say yes. Ron seems to be deep in thought, brows knitted in contemplation. Girit beckons for his attention

"There is much danger and I do not want your blood on my hands."

That's when Ron breaks out into a wide smile.

"Who am I kidding? We're in. It sounds like a blast."

Girit's eye twitches.

"Pardon?"

"We'll do what we can." Ron tells her. "On our home planet, we do not desert a friend in need."

Gamirah beams with joy. She looks as though she is about to jump to her feet and dance around the hollow.

"Don't worry about us, Elder Girit," Ron assures Girit. "My little bro' and I got this one in the bag."

A smile lights up Girit's face.

"On behalf of all my people, I thank you!" She turns to Gamirah. "Now, Gamirah, why don't you point these gentlemen towards the southern path?"

She bows her head. "It will lead you directly to Gaaqet."

Gamirah claps her hands.

"Thank you, Finn and Ron. We do not have the Galaxy Coin to pay you for your trouble, but if there's anything else we can do, please tell us."

We stand to our feet, and a wave of pride rushes over me. *Here I am, the hero, about to save these Ghahlaous'e-people in glorious butt-kicking action!*

Or at least, that's what I imagine.

GAMIRAH STANDS UP FOR HERSELF

Gamirah escorts us to Girah's edge, facing the heart of their territory and to the start of a well-trodden path covered with damp foliage. Admittedly, the forest sends a chill down my spine, but I'm high enough on my metaphorical horse to ignore the sensation.

"Go ahead, Ron. I'll be right behind you." I say and we set off down the track.

As Gamirah watches us trek into the forest, she calls out.

"Follow this path. It will lead you directly to the tree. Be careful!"

She waves, but as soon as that hand falls, I see a look of deep concern cross her face. I can't stop to question her as Ron is pushing on past the tree-line and is already nearly out of sight.

As I hurry to catch up with him, I stumble along as my foot catches in various roots and branches. We continue towards our goal, the air grows considerably thicker. My feigned confidence is starting to wane. Ron must be feeling it too because he looks back at me.

"Ya' know," he says quietly, "a smart person would say we should turn back."

"You saying I'm not smart?" I demand, my voice rising in anger.

Ron laughs.

"Just making sure we're on the same page. Meaning, we're both idiots."

Summoning the image of Girah and its citizens, I calm down.

"It's not Girit's fault her homeland isn't rich enough to afford proper help. We can't just leave them like this. I wouldn't sleep at night." I say.

Ron nods.

"I agree."

We walk until the sky darkens. Behind the twilight veil of night, millions of stars appear, and the moons cast silver beams upon the treetops. Ron's square jaw and sharp features are masked by shadows. Only his wide brown eyes and figure are visible from a distance.

Crack!

Ron marches on, unaware of the sound. I grab his equipment pack, bringing him to a halt.

"Woah, what are you..."

"Shh! Didn't you hear that? There's someone or something in the undergrowth."

We stare at a nearby clump of bushes half-concealed by looming trees. Ron's right-hand reaches for his leg pouch and pulls out a Neo Bracer.

"Who's there? Come on out!" he calls.

I half-expect a Spawn to propel itself from the bushes and bite Ron's hand off. I grab the compact-square of my plasma pistol.

"Wait!" a familiar female voice cries, and Gamirah emerges from the trees.

"Gamirah? What are you doing here? You should be back in the village." I exclaim.

She bites her lip.

"I- I know, I just..."

We re-holster our weapons, walking towards her.

"Your gunna' get yourself hurt ya' know. Why did

you follow us?" Ron demands.

She looks down at the ground to mask her expression.

"My best friend, Goorib, was part of the battalion sent to investigate Gaaqet, I've wanted to find him myself, but Elder Girit refuses. She says the role of a scholar is too important."

Ron's look is compassionate, yet firm.

"Elder Girit is correct, I understand you want to save your friend, but you have no battle experience. The tree could be capable of anything."

Gamirah is clearly distraught and her eyes fill with frustrated tears.

"Just go home." Ron tells her gently.

For the first time since we've been reunited, Ron sounds mature and fatherly. He turns, heels digging in the mud, leaving her to face his back.

"Wait a minute!"

She stomps her foot and mud squishes between her toes, leaving a deep imprint.

"Ever since the Citadel allowed us to join as a Known Planet, we've been given access to Citadel libraries. I've been reading about dark magic, wondering why we Ghahlaous'e are born from it"

She pauses, and a tear rolls down her cheek.

"I think Gaaqet is inherently evil."

I interject.

"But, even if it is, the Ghahlaous themselves aren't evil. Just because the god-tree was born from dark magic doesn't mean it's necessarily..."

Gamirah stops me.

"Please, Finn. You'll understand when you see it."

She faces me with unyielding determination.

"When we are born, Gaaqet burns into our memories the evil emanating from it. It drives some Ghahlaous mad."

She turns back to Ron.

"Take me with you. I'm a scholar. I know Gaaqet better than anybody. I'll be the one who documents the truth. The other Ghahlaous are stubborn and I need to bring Goorib back. He's my best friend. Ghahlaous aren't born with parents. Friends are all we have."

Ron hears the intensity in her voice and sees the pleading look in her eyes.
He groans.

"Augh, what kind of first-class-soldier am I?"

He throws his arms in the air.

"Right, ok, fine. You can come."

"Oh, thank you! You won't regret it, I promise you."

"Just stay close to us, and don't do anything reckless."

We continue our journey for another fifteen minutes. Ron is at the front of the line, Gamirah, now a part of our merry band of misfits, is close behind him and I bring up the rear. Gamirah remains on edge, I can tell because of her laboured breathing and irregular footsteps.

"It should be here," Gamirah's warns Ron and me, "Past those large prickle bushes."

As we approach the bushes, a strong gust of wind sweeps in, blowing the sharp spines into our path. Ron moves forward with extreme caution and I move up close so that he and I can sandwich Gamirah from the worst of the damage that they can inflict. Fortunately, our spacesuits act like armour, and we are able to press on until we break free into a clearing. My eyes widen. I can hardly believe what I am seeing.

Gaqeet towers above us, blocking the moon-lit sky. Its arm-like branches coil upwards, leeching life from nearby trees like a growing infection. The god-tree's bark is ebony, and blood-red. Large fissures split the mighty trunk into sections, revealing wounded and exposed innards. Black sap leaks from Gaqeet's wounds, dripping to the forest floor. Each hefty droplet sinks into ankle-deep mud.

Ron is equally stunned by this sight. He turns to Gamirah.

"Has it always looked like this?"

"It wasn't bleeding before." Gamirah says.

The forest is eerily quiet. Even the wind has stopped to catch its breath.

"If Goorib's platoon went missing, they aren't here now."

Both hands find his holsters, drawing his Neo Bracers.

"Stay where you are, Gamirah," Ron orders.

She reluctantly obeys, stepping into the shadows of the trees. Her grey eyes are her only discernible feature.

"Buwar..."

The sound echoes across the clearing and I stare at Ron's stomach.

"Was that you?" I ask.

His scowl answers that question.

WE GET OUR BUTTS KICKED BY A GIANT TREE

"Buwarrrr!"

The monstrous cry increases in volume, blasting my helmet's ear-pieces and causing my head to throb. Gamirah covers her ears but she is definitely also in pain.

The ground beneath my boots trembles with aftershock. Another quake causes my boot to slip into a crack, slamming my backpack against a rock before I have time to react.

"Finn!"

Ron's concerned cry pulls my attention to Gaqeet. Within its core, waves of energy crackle and snap through the air, literally causing my hair to stand on end. Ron leaps to my aid, pulling me to my feet.

I shout into my throat-mic.

"We need to get out of here!"

"Buwaaarrrr!!!!"

A high pitched, monstrous caterwaul causes both of us to cry out in pain. We backpedal from the painful screech.

"What the hell is that core in its chest!?" I shout.

"I don't know." Ron says, "but whatever it is, it certainly isn't friendly."

A series of splits run in a straight line up the bark – some wider than others. As we watch, one of them spits out hot, sticky sap the colour of tar, all over us. We wipe the dark fluid from our visors in time to see Gaqeet lift itself out of the ground, pulling on its roots.

In the center of the largest split in the trunk, a gem - dark as night - is lodged and it pulsates with energy. As we stand mesmerized by the sight, the trunk splits, revealing a mind-bending spiral, lined with rows of razor-sharp teeth, snapping and biting in our direction. Adrenaline courses through my body. *Oh ya, this is WAY worse than a Spawn attack.*

That's when I spot them. Behind Gaqeet, tucked low to the ground, is a humanoid figure. It's glowing emerald eyes meet mine. I swear I can see a thin toothed smile hidden behind the shrubbery.

"Who is that?"

My question is lost in the sea of chaos. Ron's yell breaks my trance.

"Watch out!"

A log twice the size of my body hurtles towards me. I manage to react in time. The projectile misses my helmet by about a hand's spread. On my knees, I watch helplessly as Gaqeet drags itself across the ground, leaving a trough in its wake. Tiny branches reach out, attempting to maul our faces. A branch wraps around my left foot.

This is going to test my space-suit!

The thought does little to quell the inevitable. I'm lifted off the ground. Blood rushes to the top of my head. The world becomes a twisted mess, and my back impacts the ground. I flip onto my stomach. My body tingles head-to-toe with shock and pain. In a futile attempt to slow Gaqeet, I dig my fingernails into the dirt but Gaqeet holds firm. Its immense strength pulls me towards its gaping maw.

A trio of plasma bolts whirrs past my head, breaking the dense wood. My captor squeals, the branch constraining my ankle snaps as Ron's arms wrap under my elbows, dragging me to my feet.

"I'll admit, we're a bit underprepared!" he says.

He drags me towards Gamirah. She's hiding in the trees, paralyzed by fear, but when we reach her, she grabs my hand. Her voice is shrill with concern.

"Are you ok?!"

The question brings my attention to the increasing tension on my spine.

"Sorry, no time to check," Ron says.

He shoves us both between the shoulders.

"Run now, while we can!"

We need no urging and move as fast as we can. We do little to outrun the monster's pursuit. It barrels through the woodland, smashing everything in its path and utterly destroying any life below.

"We can't outrun it!" I yell.

Ron's head twists, spotting something behind us. His mouth parts to yell a warning, but his body is already closing the gap between us. He tackles us into the ground and the three of us land in a heap. A giant log whooshes past our heads exploding a nearby canopy. Panting and wheezing, Ron scoops Gamirah into his arms bridal style.

"What are you doing?!" she demands.

"No offence, but you don't run very fast! We need to get to higher ground!"

He frantically nods to the treetops. *How will that help with stopping a thirty-foot alien-tree?!*

Blindly, I follow his order. Pinning my sights on the tallest tree I can find, I twist my hips, aiming my DPE shot. *Don't mess up, like in weapons training!* The hook thwacks into the thick bark. *That's better!* Hitting the acceleration button, my feet land squarely on the trunk. My hands are struggling to grip the nearest branch.

Pulling myself over, I glance across the path. Ron and Gamirah are also in the safety of a tree, looking down at the enemy. That's when I realize... *Gaqeet has no eyes! That's why Ron wants us in the trees! It senses vibrations!*

Confirming my theory, I study Gaqeet's roots as they scour the ground, searching for us and my eyes are drawn to its center.

What is that crystal in its chest? I stare at the dark swirling mass of power. *That's clearly what's caused it to go insane. If we stop that power source, we might win!*

One of the monsters' limbs coils around the base of Ron and Gamirah's hiding place. Ron adjusts himself, his left foot knocking against the closest branch. The slight vibration causes Gaqeets feelers to twitch. It roars and lunges, barreling against the tree ripping its roots.

Gamirah jumps to a nearby branch, slamming her ribcage then slipping. Her left hand manages to grip tight as she dangles twelve feet in the air. Ron grabs his plasma pistol and fires two beams into the enemies' thick bark, splattering sap into the leaves. The monster rears up.

"Watch out, Ron!"

It swings directly at him and I see my brother's horrified expression as the trunk slams square into his chest. The lateral blow does not tear through the armoured spacesuit, but he tumbles to the ground, landing with a heavy thwack! The front of his helmet is buried in the dirt, his eyes are shut and his hand is not moving.

"No!!" *I have to save them!*

Gaqeet twists its spine, the dark rays of its mysterious energy blasting radioactive heat. *No time to hesitate!* I fire my D.P.E, nailing its trunk. A branch rises to deal damage, but I leap into the air, reeling myself in towards the enemy. As I near it, I angle my feet, landing on one of its arms.

"Here I am ugly!"

I can feel the heat from Gaqeet's energy overcoming the cooling in my suit, which I've set to maximum, yet I hold firm. The adrenaline from watching Ron get knocked-unconscious is enough to raise a vicious-animal in me. In the corner of my eye, past the mess of tangled leaves, I spot Gamirah jumping to the ground, ducking under Gaqeet's roots. She grabs my brother by the underarms, dragging him to the nearest bush.

Shifting balance to my hips, I place one hand on Gaqeet, the other into my pocket. Fishing out my plasma pistol, I point the barrel towards Gaqeet's heart and fire.

BAM! My arm slightly recoils, muscles retracting from kickback.

"Gwarrr!!"

Gaqeet screams in agony as the brilliant-crystal chips. Within the white noise, three branches find me, wrapping around my core like a cocoon. I sail from the God-Tree in a daze, before landing in a heap on the ground. My head throbs, breathing is nearly impossible, and every muscle is on fire.

Between the olive, beige, and black blurs, Ron – now conscious again - stumbles to his feet, glaring defiance at my approaching enemy.

"Fight me, you ugly garden sprout!" he shouts.

Two powerful laser beams streak towards Gaqeet, cutting the mighty God-Tree down the middle, leaving a two-foot gash in its wake. Ron spins round with Gamirah hot on his heels. Circling around him, she leaps to help me to my feet.

"We have to hide!" she cries.

I turn in time to see Ron pivot as his leg gives out.

Slam! He face-plants into the dirt. He grabs his ankle and squeezes.

"Ron, your foot!"

"It's just a sprain!" He winces. "Keep running!"

Gaqeet is still reeling from Ron's attack. Gamirah rushes to help me drag Ron into the underbrush. My brother's injury causes us to stumble into the nearest thicket.

"We can lose it." Gamirah whispers. "Lay on your stomach, hold your breath."

Gaqeet stands where we once were, branches searching for any signs of life. I suck in a deep breath and hold it until I think I'll burst. However, it works.
Gaqeet flails around for a moment or two longer but, finding nothing but air in its path, real-

izes its prey has escaped, it continues, pulling its roots, trampling into the distance.

"We're safe for now" Gamirah mutters.

Gaqeet is now a distant rumble.

Keeping my mic volume low, I whisper to Ron.

"We need to find a way to fight that thing somehow,"

"You're right. What we need is a plan. Got any bright ideas?"

"I told you, Ron, I'm not the experienced one here. This is my first mission, or have you forgotten that?" I say angrily.

My fiery response triggers resolve within him.

"No, I most certainly haven't. Ulmu and I have placed faith in you for a reason. We could have picked any genius from Earth so why do you think we picked you?"

I'm stunned by his comments and this seeming reversal of our roles and don't know how to respond. Gamirah breaks in on our exchange.

"Uhm, guys?" Her trembling finger points towards the treetops.

"Whatever plan we have we better execute it quickly, Gaqeet is heading straight for Girah."

GIRAH GETS SOME FREE REMODELING

Mere seconds have passed, yet the monster has already managed to gain considerable distance between us and it. Groaning in pure frustration, I jump from the bushes onto the demolished path.

"It's too strong to take on alone. We need to call in reinforcements."

My depressed disposition is met with Ron's fierce determination.

"By the time they get here, it will be too late. We just need to be careful."

Ron manages to put pressure on his ankle, his lips tighten in concentration as he pushes past the pain.

"And call me crazy", he continues, "but the missing Ghahlaous might be inside that tree."

Gamirah's jaw goes slack at the suggestion. She stands up and faces my brother, her tight-knit expression urging him to continue.

"Gaqeet gifts the Ghahlaous with life; it can take it back."

The idea sends a shiver down my spine.

"It's just a hypothesis, but a likely one."

Gamirah's smoky cheeks turn white.

"Oh no, you're right." She groans. "Goorib..."

"They might still be alive," Ron assures her, placing a gentle touch on her shoulder.

"We don't know what that magic crystal is or what it's capable of, but we need to find out."

Ron begins limping down the path, waving for us to follow. It's painful to watch him stumble on one busted ankle.

"We'll doom an entire race to extinction if we blindly attack."

Gritting our teeth, we clamber over fallen trees, by-passing bushes that block our path. My back aches and my legs ache abominably from exertion.

Why does Ron have to put so much faith in me? His compliments are sincere, yet they feel like double-edged swords. *I can't solve an equation if I don't have all the variables.*

My eyes widen. *Wait, it's simple. He just said it!*

"The core-"

Excitedly, I slap Ron's shoulder catching his attention.

"It's simple," I tell him. "Like a boss battle, in a video game! We'll keep our distance, up in the tree-tops, so Gaqeet struggles to sense us. Then, we can strike at the heart with one well-aimed projectile...an Argon Bomb should do the trick!"

A huge smile cracks on Ron's face.

Numbers rush through my mind, the memory of our previous encounter forms a chart in my brain.

"Gaqeet's swinging range is roughly eighteen feet."

I flip my attention to Gamirah,

"Gamirah, you have to find a way around the tree and convince everyone there to evacuate the town. Lead your people to our transport ship."

"I'll manage it somehow," she promises and slips away into the forest.

"Finn"
The urgency in Ron's voice brings me to an

immediate halt. In the distance, the claw-like branches of our enemy glide through the treetops and we hear a chorus of screaming. Ron grits his teeth.

"I'll distract it. You go through with the plan."

"What about your ankle?" I ask him, pointing to the swollen appendage. "I should be the distraction. You won't last long."

"Gaqeet will kill you. You're untrained and inexperienced," my brother says, his voice conveying his concern. "I'm the Aver in charge of protecting you. I aim to do just that. Okay? Just don't take a coffee break." "

He pats me on the shoulder, and I see a look of grim determination through his visor.

I steady my laboured breathing.

"Ok..." I nod. "I won't let you down."

"I know."

△△△

Standing at the edge of the disaster zone, at the start of the southern path, I begin to worry about what I have taken on. Gamirah is urging the Ghahlaous citizens who swarm like ants, desperately trying to escape their homes.

"Into the Western Wood! There is safety in the Western Wood," she repeats. "Run now!"

Handfuls of Ghahlaous clear the area. Those few that are left have injuries too severe to vacate them in a hurry. They drag themselves undercover. The carnage makes my stomach twist. *Is this the best we can do?*

Clearing out the main paths, Gaqeet swings one of its many branches, twisting around a house with unbelievable strength and digging into the bark. Debris from the demolished homes smothers the crops and flowerbeds so carefully set out by the Ghahlaous. The rope bridges snap like rubber bands. Multiple Ghahlaous citizens are caught under the roots, suffocating beneath its sheer mass. *I can hardly even fire my D.P.E! How am I supposed to land a sniper-shot into its core?!* "

"What are we waiting for?" Ron barks.

He begins jogging in place. Gamirah circles to face us as it detects our movement.

Behind him, I spot a mighty oak-like tree. *It's the perfect vantage point.*

"You're right, let's do this." I say.

"That's the spirit."

Tip-toeing a few paces, I cross the path, tucking

behind a fallen Ghahlaous'e home, fallen leaves and petals sticking to my muddy suit. Ron begins his distraction, charging into the fray, stomping on the ground like a child having a tantrum.

"Hey!"

Ron's arms wave frantically through the air.

"Over here you son-of-a-shrub!"

It takes one second for Gaqeet to see my brother as the main threat. The god-tree roars in defiance.

Alright, Gaqeet is distracted. Now's my chance. Turning, I fire my D.P.E, zooming up into the tree, pushing past a mess of foliage. I manage to land with both feet on a branch.

"You couldn't hit a bug if it was sleepin' on your nose!" Ron's shouts, his voice amplified by the external speaker buds on our space-suits.

His voice draws my attention away from the struggling victims. A wooden arm lumbers towards my brother, he ducks dodging the appendage with ease. He uses the audio alarm to let loose an ear-piercing whistle. Gaqeet's bark twists, revealing it's blackened heart lodged between the diamond-shaped crystal. I can sense the beast's rising irritation. Ron continues to mock the creature.

"Is that the best you can do!?"

Maybe he's going a bit too far? Suddenly, I remember the special glasses Ulmu gave me. *I can copy Ron's attack patterns! That will double my chances in landing a critical-hit.*

"Activate glasses" I say, praying that the glasses are integrated into the suit's AI pack.

Immediately, a blue light-beam coats Ron with a subtle outline, following his every movement and storing it away into the AI's memory. A young female A.I, much like Eunoia, whispers in my ear. *"Pattern detected, storing into the database."*

The second attack comes bolting towards Ron's face. He crouches as it narrowly misses his helmet. He plants his good foot on a root. Like an acrobat on a tightrope, Ron teeters before leaping with all his might. Unfortunately, he gains little height. His face is contorted with concentration and pain. Un-holstering his bracers, he slices a V shape, leaving an unimpressive mark on the base of the god's spine.

A swear-word forms on his lips as he's knocked off the root, spiralling through the air and tumbling onto the reed-covered roof of a nearby, still intact, building. His limbs flail, trying to find something to grab onto, but they only dig into the dirt.

I still can't get a good shot! Spotting a nearby Ghahlaous building that's also still intact, I leap, attempting to get an adequate opening to attack. My landing is far more graceful. *I might be getting the hang of this.*

Again, the creature moves erratically, its attention continually shifting between Ron and the remaining citizens. Inside the collapsed home, Ron's bloody fingers curl around a rock and he pulls himself up, but it is obvious that he is weakening.

Through his visor I can see blood trickling from a cut on his forehead. The situation has become desperate. I reach into my pocket, finding the base of the Argon Bomb. *If an opening isn't created soon, I'll have no choice but to jump into action.* The idea of dying on my first mission is not a pleasant thought.

Gaqeet raises five branches, spinning them together to form a malformed fist. My brother pulls himself from the den, eyes fraught with rising concern. He moves, trying to find a defensive position, but his leg gives out, pushing him to his knees. Twisting, he fires his D.P.E straight into my tree.

The god-tree's fist catapults towards him but Ron skids out of the way like a car drifting on a racetrack as he triggers the DPE twice which reels him in double-time. But he gets wrapped up in the line. Looking down at him just below me, *I know that it's now or never!*

My glasses beep. *"Move pattern, Ron Bates, memorized."*

Gaqeet turns around, it's attention dead-set on my vulnerable brother wrapped up like a Christmas gift. All of the god-trees branches rise towards us, revealing the heart in all its horrific glory.

"Access file! Ron Bates!"

"Ron Bates confirmed."

A slew of lightning-fast information explodes into my brain. With no further hesitation, I launch from my sanctuary. Sling-shotting through the open air, my quick reflexes square my feet meeting the heart head-on.

SLAM! The energy-core once again whips against my helmet like a tornado.

"GWUAR!"

Gaqeet screeches in confusion; branches rush to defend itself from every direction. My world moves in slow-motion, every sensation alive and beating. The Argon Bombs cover flicks open between my thumb, revealing a bright blue button, the colour a pulsing dot on my ledger.

"Eat this!"

Raising my arm, I force-feed the bomb into the heart; it sucks me up to my elbow like a vacuum. My muscles tighten, blood pumping as I try to pull back, breaking from Gaqeet's powerful suction. Unhanding the bomb, my arm finally rips free. Even with the protection of my armoured suit, every tendon feels like it's been scraped with a dull knife. For what feels like an eternity, the black crystal kicks and punches at Gaqeet's insides.

My vision fades into darkness. Everything falls silent...

Am I ...dead?

Tick...

I suck hot air into my lungs. In the distance, a desperate voice screams.

"Finn! Jump!"

The darkness lightens and I see the crystal spiraling like a teetotum, I'm hypnotized...

"Tick.."

"Let go, or you'll die!!"

Ron?

Self-awareness trickles in.

That's right...I need to trust him!!

Causing my body to go limp, I fall backwards then roll to propel myself straight downwards. Arms wrap around my core, turning the world into a tumbling mess as I hit the ground.

What just happened? Where am I!?

I'm face-down in the dirt. I piece together that Ron caught me mid-fall. His arms are desperately wrapped around my shoulders. Behind him, flailing branches and roots swish through the air, clinging to life.

The bomb is about to explode! Ron shields me, enveloping me in blackness.

BOOM!

A max-level earthquake accompanied by a blast of wind blows around us, rocking us on our precarious perch. My eyes now wide open, I watch as the fuel from the argon bomb causes streams of fire to cascade up Gaqeet's body.

Gaqeet projectile-vomits the crystal from its core. Sparks of dying energy crackle through the air, hurtling it into nearby undergrowth. The tree continues to writhe and screech like a beached squid, struggling to find air.

Suddenly, it tremors from its roots up, stiffening the tree like a statue. The dying flames illuminate the town orangish-red. The God-tree remains still.

We stare at the blackened trunk for a long time but there is no sign of life

"Did we win?" I stammer.

TURNS OUT, I'M A CRAZY PERSON

"I think we did," Ron mumbles, his tangled D.P.E still resting by his feet. He reels it in as I examine the chaos.

Girah is silent as the dead. Ghahlaous'e citizens are scattered amongst the debris. Many lay wounded, staring at their destroyed city with defeated expressions. My stomach twists.

It must feel so terrible to lose your home.

A young Ghahlous'e woman wearing an amber-leaf dress rummages through debris searching for something. Silver-droplets roll slowly down her dark-grey skin.

This doesn't feel like a win...

"Finn! Ron!"

Gamirah hurtles towards us from the Western

Wood. Her arms find our shoulders as she addresses both of us, her voice rushing with excitement.

"I managed to get most of my people to the ship. Did you...?"

Her joyous chatter is cut short. I watch with increasing sadness as her large dark eyes become filled with sorrow. My eyes take in the destroyed undergrowth. I am unable to meet her gaze.

"Where is Goorib?" she asks. "And the other Ghahlaous'e men? Did Gaqeet bring them back?"

My eyes flicker up to the god-tree; *it's impossible to bring myself to tell her the truth; it's too painful...*

"I'm sorry." Ron says sadly. "I guess, once Gaqeet takes them..."

*It won't give them back...*but I presume she already knows.

She bolts forward, kicking up mud and staining the bottom of her beautiful dress. Facing the incinerated tree, she throws her fists in the air.

"Give them back!" Her voice breaks. "Please–" Other citizens stare at their scholar, visibly tongue-tied.

"You owe us! We saved you. Now give them back!"

Gamirah's weeping is met with deafening silence. She collapses to her knees.

Ron crosses the battlefield. He gazes gently into her beautiful, tear-filled eyes.

"I'm sorry, Gamirah,"

Getting on his knees beside her, Ron pulls her into a side embrace. Gamirah's head collapses into the crook of my brother's neck, tears streaking the mud on his helmet.

"We can't bring them back; I truly, wish we could..."

Ron's voice breaks. His face stiffens, yet he manages to contain his tears.

"You...did what you could." Gamirah manages.

Her hands cover her face as Ron supports her. The burden of her lost companions is too heavy to bear.

Screw-this, it's unfair!, My own tears are threatening to spill over, ones of frustration filled misery. *We did what we could and defeated the enemy, but it's still not enough. Is this what being a soldier means?*

"F i n n."

My world unexpectedly tips. Ron and Gamirah now at a ninety-degree angle. Gamirah's crying is the backdrop for my sudden descent into delirium. The millions of pores on my skin open, cold sweat soaking the inside of my suit, making me sticky and uncomfortable. *What is happening?!* I'm trembling, frozen in place. It's as if a ghost has possessed my body. My mind is my own, yet my muscles refuse to respond.

H- help me...Ron!

My vision blurs. I'm standing in the destroyed city, but ghostly shadows replace the detailed figures of my brother and Gamirah.

"D o y o u r e m e m b e r m e?"

A shaft of dark energy projects from the undergrowth—*the crystal?*

My body moves against my will, crossing the path. I thrust face-first into the entanglement of leaves. My hands are monstrous claws digging for the mysterious object.

"F i n d m e..."

It's calling for me, controlling me, like it did Gaqeet! The revelation of what's happening does little to ease my hysteria. I wish I could hear my heart or feel the dirt beneath my nails, but there is nothing but numbness and greed.

I need it! I'm too weak to fight back!

I think my lips twist into a wicked grin...a cackle forming in the center of my chest.

"*F i n n*" An impelling male voice whispers my name as a supernatural force pulls my hand closer.

"*Y o u a r e h i d i n g s o m e t h i n g.*"

My body involuntarily jolts forward, grabbing the crystal tightly in my hand. *What do you think I'm hiding?* I ask the crystal telepathically. *Tell me what you're talking about!*

My fingers twine around the shard. Deep within its dark material, white flecks resembling stars crisscross in hypnotic patterns. Fear runs through me, yet I hold tight; the crystal pulls me deeper. Sinking into the void, my mind engages with infinity.

"*W h o a r e y o u r e a l l y?*"

I respond with confusion. *My name is Finn Bates, I'm a human, from earth.*

"*L I A R*"

"Yo' Finn, are you ok?"

The crystal ejects me from the mental-black-hole, I'm devoid of all thought...*Whatever this evil object is...it's in control of me now.*

The world remains a blur, as my legs involuntarily flinch. I rise to my feet, spinning to face my brother. Gamirah hangs close behind, wiping her lingering tears. Ron's eyes thin, glaring at the object in my grasp.

"What are you doing? That could be dangerous. We don't know what it is."

"I t s f i n e"

"It's fine."

The crystal's words are my own. My inner determination is too weak to fight back.

"W e s h o u l d l e a v e"

"We should leave."

My voice trembles. Ron gives a reluctant head nod. *No! I'm trapped! Help me!* But the crystal has my lips sewn shut. Gamirah circles beside my brother, her eyes still thick with tears.

"The rest of my people are at your transport ship. We should go."

"S h e ' s r i g h t"

"She's right." I hear myself say.

My right foot moves forward, lifting me over the bushes. Like a puppet, I am moved to the entrance of the western wood while Ron and Gamirah follow. My head's lopsided and swinging which makes me motion sick. My stomach twists. Turning I scream. *Help me let go of the crystal! I need to set myself free!* Yet my grip is solid as iron...

"Are you ok?" Ron's question sounds distant. "You're pale as a ghost..."

Ensuring Gamirah isn't listening, he whispers.

"I know things look bleak right now, but we've done something good here. I promise."

His words are almost lost against a sea of black-noise, as if my spirit is detached from my body.

"t e l l m e w h a t y o u r h i d i n g F i n n"

I'm not hiding anything! I retort. *When I was six, I stole a chocolate bar from the convenience store, but that's no cause to control my mind!* The crystal responds with maniacal laughter; it circles my head, sending tingles down my spine. *Please, let me go!*

"n o !"

My brother's hand is a blur waving across my limited vision, but I am miles away.

"Hello, earth to Finn?"

I swallow. *Ron, take the crystal away from me for flips-sake!*

"a c c e p t m e"

My breath catches in my lungs. That's when the crystal is ripped from my hands. Everything turns clear. The world flips to face me, blood rushes to my face. I gasp. Faster than a speeding bullet, Ron has his arms on my shoulders, supporting me as my legs go limp. *Am I...safe?*

Ron's distraught eyes look down at the crystal in his hand.

"Don't touch it!"

My arms tremble, body coursing with adrenaline. "It'll control your mind!" I scream.

"Hey, hey, it's ok, nothing is happening," my brother says while checking my expression. "Are you really ok? What happened to you?"

My mind struggles for words.

"I-" my heart returns to its usual pace. "-it was talking to me."

"The crystal?"

Gamirah tries desperately to pull information from me.

"What did it say? Did it hurt you?"

"It called out to me...it controlled my mind, even before I held it in my hand"

My fingers flex, emotion working into every syllable.

"My mind wasn't my own. I couldn't fight it off."

Gamirah stammers.

"But we didn't hear anything." *That's impossible...why just me?*

Ron grunts in disapproval.

"I should have paid more attention. I'm sorry. We'll talk more later. We need to contact Girit, and get back to Euonia to get our wounds healed. If this crystal starts talking, I'll let ya' know."

So, I'm just crazy? Ron must sense my overwhelming stress.

"Let's just focus on the mission, one step atta' time, bro."

GIRIT GIVES ME A SOLID PEP-TALK

Elder Girit is the first to spot us making our way through the tree-line, elbowing aside tufts of branches. Her right hand is caringly wrapped around an injured citizen. She raises it to greet us. Gamirah makes a mad dash across the clearing, collapsing into Girit's open arms, further tears running down the scholars' cheek.

"My dear Gamirah!"

Girit rubs her hand against the younger Ghahlaouse's back.

"Why are you crying?"

"They're dead," Gamirah replies. "Goorib and the others. Gaaqet took them. They're never coming back."

"And what of us?" the elder Ghahlaous replies

matter-of-factly. "Goorib and his platoon knew what they were sacrificing when they ventured into the wood."

She gestures to her citizens, crouching close to the ground beneath Eunoia's metal wings.

"Meanwhile, look at our people, who would be dead as well..."

She points at my brother and me.

"...If not for them."

She's...thanking us? My jaw turns slack in amazement. *How is this possible?* Girit rises to her feet, leaving Gamirah crouched on the ground, her hands digging into the dirt.

"I don't understand."

Girit faces me with a warm smile.

"What do you not understand Finn? You've saved my people."

"Girah is destroyed." I say sorrowfully.

My guilt has begun to manifest as sorrow.

"We can rebuild." Girit says.

"Your men are dead." I insist.

"It was not you who killed them. If you two had not so bravely taken on this task, we would have been destroyed entirely!"

Girit's voice rises to a commanding volume as she turns to address her citizens. They rise to their feet.

"If not for Finn and Ron, we would all be at the mercy of Gaaqet!"

Gamirah's chest rises and falls.

"Elder Girit is right!"

The scholar stands, holding her fist once more into the air.

"They saved us!"

A chorus of cheers resounds throughout the clearing.

Ron's hand finds my shoulder, giving a squeeze.

"See?" he says.

"I- I thought we failed and you would be angry at us, elder Girit."

"Dear child, you have done what millions would not. Put your life on the line to assist those in need. Now, smile!"

I can't refuse. I grin, and with this gesture, all feelings of doubt disappear.

"What about me?" Ron asks.

Girit gives a soft chuckle.

"Listen, Ron Bates, you fought bravely. I am honoured to call you a friend. If ever the Citadel needs our aid, we will answer the call. We are in your debt."

One last round of cheers gives me the assurance I need. Finding Gamirah, she smiles, her hands clasped over her heart. A small tear lingers in her left eye...

I know deep down; she is mourning the loss of her beloved friend.

THIS ISN'T THE END, IS IT?!

Ron and I are about to board Eunoia when a voice calls out to us.

"Finn, Ron, wait!"

We turn towards the western path. Gamirah is in a stunning summer dress stitched with brown weeds. Her bare feet skid to a halt in front of us.

"You're leaving without saying goodbye?"

I step off the metal platform.

"We are under orders to return to Altair. Gamirah, I'm so sorry about Goorib."

To my surprise, she smiles, shaking her head.

"Why are you so hard on yourself?"

Gamirah tiptoes forward. We are mere inches away from one another.

"Finn, you were so brave, not to mention super cool."

It seems that her bubbly excitement from when we first met, is restored.

"Heh, it's no big deal."

I feel a warmth turning my ears pink. Gamirah's stunning black eyes look like twilight...*W, wait! I haven't been this close to a girl my entire life!*

"Remember when I told you I wanted to study Gaaqet? Well, I've made a decision! I'm going to join the Citadel and become a file-keeper!"

I had no idea a position like that even existed...

"Gamirah, that's amazing."

With her up-close, I can see light freckles around her dimples. Her lips purse, amusement alight in her expression.

"I'll discover the truth behind that crystal as well, no matter what. For Goorib, and the rest of his platoon."

She smiles.

"I have lots of studying to do though, so don't expect to see me anytime soon. But you will see me again, I promise."

With that, she leans in, planting a cool kiss on

my right cheek. She lingers, seeming to enjoy the moment while I flush head to toe, stammering my reply like a sixth-grader.

"T, that's so cool! G- good luck."

Gamirah dances off the platform, landing gracefully in the mud. She giggles, turning on her heels, raises her hand in a goodbye wave to Ron and then sets off back towards Girah.

"Bye, Ron, thanks for everything you've done for us!" she calls

"No kiss for me?"

They laugh as the tail of her dress disappears behind a tree.

"She was nice." Ron says pointedly, looking at me.

"Don't bother trying to get me together with her." I warn him.

He gives a hearty laugh, pushing me towards the air-lock.

"You're a big-boy now Finn., You don't need your big-bro to hook you up with the ladies."

I ignore him and we board Euonia. The ramp retracts and the airlock restores earth-normal atmosphere throughout the ship.

Admittedly, departing Creyenia leaves a hole in my heart. *This is the first time I've completed a task as an Aster.*

This first mission will forever remain in my memories.

Sometime later, we spread out on the couches in Eunoia's crew lounge, having treated our bruises and cuts. We were fortunate that our suits protected us from worse injuries, although Ron's ankle is now tightly bandaged.

Through the viewport, we can see the rays of distant sunlight warming the ground. We're alone, staring out into the Creyenia western wood, contemplating the results of our mission.

"Tell you what, Ron, I'm not sorry to go back to HQ and catch up on some sleep."

Ron gives a thoughtful nod.

"I'm not surprised. You outdid yourself, Finn. I'm impressed."

I tuck my knees up to my chin.

"I didn't do enough though. Goorib is still dead."

"Girit told you, Finn. That's not your fault"

"I know," I point at Ron's pouch. "It's that thing."

Ron clicks the pouch open,

"Almost forgot I had it. Guess we need to hand it over to The Citadel"

Strangely, he sounds disappointed at the prospect of parting with the artifact. My heart races as he shows the crystal on his bare hand.

"What is it?" he muses

"I don't know."

He glares deep into the recess of its swirling-pools.

"As far as I'm aware, The Citadel has no records of Magical Crystals that turn things evil. Did you really hear a voice?"

The memory is still vivid in my mind.

"You don't believe me?" I challenge.

"Come on, of course I do."

He flips the crystal in his hand.

"I just don't hear anything. It looks like a regular ol' rock."

Right on cue, a whisper coils from the recess of my mind...

"f i n n ..."

The voice disappears like a bad dream, I lick my drying lips in worry.

"It controlled me. I don't know how or why, but it did."

"I wonder why only you?"

His sincere reply causes me to question myself; *maybe it was just stress from the battle?* Yet I can hear the mysterious voice so clearly.

"What did it say?" Ron asks.

It kept saying, *"Tell me what you're hiding."* When I said 'nothing' it called me a *"liar"*

The questions have many implications. *Is it because I'm hiding mom and dad's divorce?* I can't figure out the answer...

"Everything was a blur so I can't remember; it was a male voice, though."

I recall the pair of green eyes I saw in the forest, *was that just a figment of my imagination? It must have been.*

"Interesting."

A moment of awkward silence passes. In the corner of my vision, Ron flexes his fists, pushing the crystal into his pouch.

"Can I ask you a question? It's about mom and dad."

Oh, no... "Sure."

His Jericho Watch lights up. *A diversion, thank you!*

"It's a transmission from Ulmu." Ron accepts the incoming message.

Ping!

A blue projection appears. A light blue hue blankets the Godsonion down to his shoulders.

"Hey, boss-man." Ron grins. "Don't worry; we're still alive."

"I can see that."

Ulmu's hologram quivers.

"I called to instruct you that we need you both back at HQ immediately."

"Why tha' rush?"

"Multiple Raider ships and Spawn swarms have been noted within the K-A galaxy. We fear an encounter with a single party would spell disaster for the both of you. The Citadel, additionally, wishes to speak with Finn."

A wave of uneasiness makes me gulp. Ron salutes.

"Copy that El' Capitan. We're comin' home."

Ulmu frowns.

"When you return, don't forget to write your mission statements."

Ron's eyes roll.

"If I have to track you down for missing paperwork, Mr. Bates, I swear …"

Ron ends the call, Ulmu's threat falling on deaf ears.

"Alright, time to haul off."

My brother rises to his feet, his ankle twists, causing a spasm of pain.

"Augh!" he gasps.

Gripping Ron's shoulder, I steady him, leaning him against Eunoia's hull.

"Thanks dude! We're in pretty bad shape, huh?

"We'll make it. Come on."

I help him to the ladder and help him climb it using one foot and his arms to pull himself up. I follow and we take our accustomed places on the flight deck as Ron has EON set us on our way to Altair. Eunoia's thrusters come online, throwing-up distant leaves and twigs.

Once we're on our way, Ron grins at me.

"I'm betting that Naki missed you."

Tapping my foot, I roll-my-eyes in frustration

"Ron, I warned you! Stop teasing me about Naki.

You told me that I don't need my brother to arrange dates for me."

"You don't," he replies...still grinning.

"Well then, stop teasing me about Naki."

He shrugs.

"Naki who?" he asks.

EON's voice prevents further discussion on that topic.

"Initiating hyperdrive."

Relaxing in my seat, I kick up my feet, releasing tension from my lower back and hips.

Ron closes his eyes, exhaustion finally taking over. Then, right out of the blue, Ron looks at me.

"Mom and Dad have split up, haven't they?"

W- what, did he just say?!

A wave of nausea curdles my stomach. I'm shocked to find a look of understanding on his face.

"What do you mean split? L- like divorced?" I fake a chuckle. "As if!"

Ron's smile is partial.

"Come on, man, you and I both know that the only thing Mom and Dad have in common is their love of raising their kids. With me missing, n' you all grown up, they wouldn't last long."

"You don't know that." I say.

"Yes, I do."

"They could still get back together; we could fix…"

Ron's voice breaks into frustration.

"It's not your job to fix their relationship, Finn."

"Then what should I do!?"

My shout of exasperation occurs as EON takes us out of hyperdrive. Altair is floating in the distance

Ron's eyes remain glued to mine, thoughtful yet simultaneously stern.

"I don't know," Ron admits, "but I won't feign ignorance and pretend that everything will go back to normal if I return."

My heart is racing a mile-a-minute. *If Ron knows the truth about Mom and Dad, will he give up on coming home?* The anxiety is a knife in my gut.

"But Ron, if we make Earth a known planet, Mom and Dad could get back together!"

"I told you already, Finn. I'm not making the earth a Known Planet for the family. I'm doing it for humanity."

Hearing him say this, I'm reminded of people like Chad Brunestick and his friends. *Do bullies like them deserve a better life?* My lips tremble, overwhelmed by everything that's happened over the last week.

"Ron, are you angry at me for lying?"

He shakes his head.

"No, of course not. I'm the one who lied."

He crosses his arms, staring out into space reminiscing.

"When I landed on earth, I checked up on Mom and Dad; I had to see em'"

His voice cracks.

"I knew right away that their relationship was broken beyond repair."

"Oh..."

I'm stunned. Ron's eyes squeeze tight.

"I didn't want to upset you, Finn. You're already dealing with a lot."

That's when it hits me. I've been utterly unaware of Ron's empathy towards my situation; I *should have told him the truth.*

"Ron," I say with renewed determination, "we're

going to make the earth a Known Planet, together."

"Heck ya-"

He reaches into his pocket, fishing out the mystifying gem.

"And now, we've got one doozy of a mystery to solve."

A new wave of optimism surges through me. The tantalizing mystery of this magic crystal, the joy of meeting new friends, and the eagerness to learn new things.

I wouldn't miss it in a million years.

AFTERWORD

Please leave a review on...

Amazon.ca

OR

@ www.parisauthor.com

BOOKS IN THIS SERIES
HYPERNOVA SERIES

Mystery Of Planet Creyenia: Book 1

When Finn was twelve years old, his elder brother, Ron, disappeared without a trace. Five years later he's back and needs Finn's help in an astronomical way. Ron has become a member of the Citadel, a collection of the universes, smartest extraterrestrial beings who voyage between worlds and galaxies saving lives. Ron is having trouble finding a teammate, and thinks his brother is the perfect fit. Finn accepts the role for personal reasons and is thrown into a catastrophic world filled with adventure and peril.

Worlds At War: Book 2

"Finn Bates and Ron Bates are members of The Citadel, a collection of the smartest extraterrestrial beings in the Known Galaxies. After an intrepid adventure to the planet Creyenia, they discovered a mysterious crystal that infects living beings with tremendous magical energy...while also turning them insane. They need to discover the truth behind this bewildering gem. Unfortunately, that isn't the only problem on their plates.Odium, leader of the Raiders and controller of Spawn, has launched several attacks on Known Planets. His aim is to trigger a bloody-war that lasts for millenials to come. It's up to our heroes to stop him. Once and for all. By whatever means necessary."

Odiums Revenge: Book 3

Coming April 1st, 2022

PRAISE FOR AUTHOR

"Would highly recommend for any young adult reader. Space, action, family, and blossoming romance. Great little adventure escape!"

- ANGELA, AMAZON REVIEWS

"The writer is very expressive and vibrant. A fun story that took me back to my teens and the world of fantasy, travel and making new friends."

- W. HUNT, AMAZON REVIEWS

"I kept wanting to pick it up and read more! Fantasic, can't wait for the next one."

- HEATHER, FACEBOOK REVIEWS

"This book is really difficult to put down once you start it, the author did a very good job in creating the start of what could be a very big universe of stories, potentially several series at least, I look forward to book 2"

- ALEX REI, AMAZON REVIEWS

"Loved this book. Blew through it in no time. Just picked up book 2 in the series ; Worlds At War. Can't wait to dig in. Please keep em coming."

- DAN, AMAZON REVIEWS

ACKNOWLEDGEMENT

Thank you, Terry for working day in and out to edit my messy, half-sober writings.

Thank you, Aj for helping me narrow down my insane ramblings into a digestible story.

Antonio Cesar, you are the best artist I could ask for. Thank you for tranforming my strange sketches into amazing book cover(s)

Finally, my dear Bryce Fillion. You are the love of my life, thank you for letting me hog the computer everyday. You shall never play desktop-games ever again.

Made in the USA
Columbia, SC
17 April 2022